When It's True

Also by Barbara L. Murphy

Two Lives, One Heart

When It's True

To Willa,

Thank you for your support!

[signature]

Barbara Lynn Murphy

Desert Palm Press

When It's True

By Barbara L. Murphy

©2023 Barbara L. Murphy

ISBN (book) 9781954213678
ISBN (epub) 9781954213685

For permission requests, write to the publisher at lee@desertpalmpress.com or "Attention: Permissions Coordinator," at

Desert Palm Press
1961 Main Street, Suite 220
Watsonville, California 95076
www.desertpalmpress.com

Editor: Toni Kelley
Cover Design: Mich Brodeur eeboxWORX

Printed in the United States o
f America
First Edition May 2023

Acknowledgements

Lee Fitzsimmons and Desert Palm Press, thank you for bearing with me as I learn how this whole publishing process works. Your confidence in this, my sophomore effort, has helped to quiet the 'imposter syndrome' voices in my head.

I would like to thank my family and friends, who've supported my new writing career more than I ever could have anticipated.

Toni Kelley, thank you for your editing expertise and for tolerating my bad habits, which I'm sure are more than just a little annoying.

Michelle Brodeur, thank you for your beautiful cover art. I love it.

Dedication

For my wife, Nancy, who helps with this little hobby of mine more than she realizes.

Chapter One

THE BASEBALL GAME ENDED, and I switched off the television mounted on the shadowed bedroom wall. I was hopeful sleep would come quickly, but I knew that was unlikely, given my thoughts spinning like the gears I pictured in my brain. Each rotating cog fit like a puzzle piece into the wheel next to it as it turned incessantly, carrying useless thoughts from one compartment of my mind to the next. One of those thoughts was resentment that my wife Kelly, just inches away from me, fell asleep in about six and a half seconds. Next to her—or rather, I should say scattered about the king-size bed and shedding all over the lavender-shaded duvet—our two dogs were breathing heavily in various stages of REM sleep and doggie dreams. I've often wished I lived the life of one of my dogs. Their only concerns were how many treats they would get during the course of a day and whether they would suffer the horror of being forced to go outside in the rain. I'd take that kind of "stress" any day of the week, thank you very much.

Tonight's episode of sleeplessness was caused by the news I'd received earlier in the day that my ex-girlfriend would be coming into town for the holidays, and would I mind if she crashed at our house for a few days. I had not shared that bit of news with the wife. Maybe that's why she was sleeping soundly, and I was wide awake. It's not that she would mind entertaining our house guest—she knew all my ex-girlfriends and graciously indulged me in my desire to remain friends with them—but in this case, the impending visitor had just broken up with her latest girl-toy and finally expressed a desire to settle down and have a real relationship.

Oh, and she would like that 'settling down' process to be with *me*. That part had also not yet been shared with the wife. I pulled the covers over my head, breathed a deep sigh that would have made my dearly departed grandmother, an Olympic gold medal winning sigher, proud, and spent the next three hours debating my options.

* * * *

I staggered down the stairs the following morning in desperate need of a strong cup of coffee. My wife had already tended to the hounds several hours earlier, and since she was way ahead of me on the caffeine scale, she was ready to tackle the conversations of the day. On the other hand, I felt somewhat less inclined and begged for some time to allow my brain to kick into gear. Mercifully, she obliged and talked to the dogs instead. They listened better than I do anyway. After an hour or so, I assessed Kelly's mood and decided she was in the right frame of mind to hear the news without throwing a large object at me from across the room.

"Hey, babe?" I said, somewhat sheepishly.

"Yeah?" She was sitting at the kitchen table, and she looked up from her crossword puzzle.

"Um…I got a call from Jackie yesterday. She says hello."

"Oh, that's nice. How is she? And how's that very young girl she's dating? She's practically still in middle school, right?" Her eyes darted back to her puzzle, Jackie being only a mildly interesting subject for her.

I made my way to the coffee pot, grabbed the carafe and filled both of our mugs. "She's not quite that young, but close. She's twenty. And they broke up." I sat down next to her at the table.

"I'm sorry to hear that. Jackie seemed to be into her."

"She was into the great sex, but beyond that, I'm skeptical. I think I might be right because she said she was growing weary of *just* having great sex."

That must have piqued Kelly's interest because she pushed her puzzle aside to focus on me. "That doesn't sound like Jackie. Has she been abducted and replaced with an imposter? Since when is she weary of sex—especially *great* sex?"

"She says she thinks maybe she's finally growing up and wants more."

"Well, that's nice. You'd think thirty-five years old is a tad late for growing up, but who am I to judge?" Kelly's sarcasm was not well masked, as usual. "Remind me again. How old were you two when you dated?"

"I was twenty-seven, and she was twenty-four. If you think she's immature now, you should have seen her back then. It's why we broke up. Well, that and the fact that she cheated on me."

"I would think that would factor into your decision." She smiled as she stated the obvious.

I hesitated before adding the next part. "So, um…as she's telling me this story about breaking up with Ashley and maturing and growing up, blah, blah, blah, she starts to get emotional. I can hear it in her voice on the phone. At first, I thought she was just sad about forfeiting all that great sex, but then, she kinda dropped a bomb on me." I got up from our kitchen table and started a slow pace around the room while I

2

searched for the words least likely to cause an outburst from Kelly.

"Okay, so enlighten me. Whatever it is, it's obviously got you rattled because your body language just got all twitchy and weird."

"Yeah. I know." I leaned against the granite-topped counter on the island, trying not to be twitchy and weird, but without much success. "She said she thinks it's time for her to settle down."

"Okay, well, there's nothing wrong with that, per se. Seems like a good idea, right?"

"You may not think so in a few seconds when I finish the story."

"Beth, you're stalling. Spit it out, please."

"She wants to settle down *with me*. Oh, and she also wants to come and stay here for a few days during the holidays." I scrunched up my face as I finished the sentence, clearly preparing for the worst.

"I see. Well, that's an interesting turn of events. Maybe she really *has* been abducted because the Jackie I know is well aware that you are a married woman." I could tell she was getting understandably frustrated with this conversation.

"She's aware."

"Oh, so I guess that doesn't mean anything to her?" Kelly's voice began to rise, and now *she* was getting twitchy and weird. "Does it mean anything to you?"

"Of course it does, babe."

"Well, did you tell her that?" Her arms flailed as she spoke.

"Of course I did! I reminded her that I am not only married but *happily* married, and she has exactly a zero percent chance of getting back together with me."

"And did you also tell her that while sex with you is wonderful, you're no longer twenty years old?"

"Hey! That's below the belt. Was that necessary? I haven't done anything wrong here. So why am I the one getting shit for it?"

"I'm sorry. You're right. That was uncalled for." She walked over to me at the counter and put her arms around my waist.

"You know, I could have just told her no and not even mentioned the conversation to you. You'd have been none the wiser, but I thought you should know."

"Thanks, honey. I do appreciate that. I guess you caught me off guard."

"Well, she sure caught me off guard. It took me a few minutes to wrap my head around what she was saying."

"What exactly did she say?"

"She said she's been doing a lot of thinking and has realized that while everyone around her seems to be making important commitments, she's just fucking around. I think her dad's death last month hit her quite hard. Maybe it's just the grief talking. Or maybe she truly is ready to grow up, but either way, she's not doing it with me. I'll support her as a friend, but that's the extent of it."

"So, what about this request to stay here over the holidays? What do we do about that?"

"That one is completely up to you. I understand if it would be too uncomfortable, but I hope you know you have nothing to worry about." I put my arms around her neck and leaned close enough to steal a kiss as soon as the opportunity presented itself.

"I'm almost tempted to say yes just to see how the hell she plans to navigate around the two of us. Do you think she's counting on you not telling me about this little conversation?"

"No. I told her flat out I would be telling you. We don't keep secrets like that from each other."

Kelly put her hands on my cheeks and leaned in for a passionate kiss. "No, we don't. And let me remind you that only *I* can kiss you like that."

"Mmm...that is true. You can remind me a little more if you like, maybe back upstairs in the bedroom?"

"Nope. I'm not taking you to bed with thoughts of Jackie lingering in the air. Maybe later when you've forgotten all about her. In the meantime, go ahead and call her and tell her she can stay here. This should be interesting." She sat back down and finished her crossword puzzle.

Chapter Two

I WASN'T SURPRISED IN the slightest when my cell phone rang first thing the following day. Kelly and I were still lying in bed, Sunday morning snuggling with each other and the pups. I looked over at her to see if she'd rather I decline the call and deal with it later. I got the 'go ahead and answer it' face, with a little smile that told me she was anxious to see how this would play out. We both propped ourselves up on the oversized pillows. I took a deep breath and pressed the *Answer* button on my phone.

"Isn't it a little early for you, Jackie? As I recall, your Saturday nights often turn into late Sunday morning cavorting with the prettiest girl from the bar that night. Have you hit a dry spell?"

"Very funny, and good morning to you too. I told you, I'm putting that life behind me now."

"Oh really? Does that mean you didn't have company last night?"

Jackie hesitated and cleared her throat before fessing up. "Well, no, not exactly. It means I don't have company *now*. She left a few hours ago." I laughed but decided against making a more significant thing out of it—no point in poking the bear. "I got your message yesterday. Where's your wife?"

"Right here next to me in bed."

Kelly smiled and leaned in closer.

"Ah, so I guess she can hear me, huh?"

"Yep."

"Okay, then I won't say what I was gonna say about our conversation the other day."

"Jackie, you can say whatever you like. I told her everything about our conversation, just like I said I would."

"You take those marriage vows of honesty and fidelity seriously, don't you?"

"I think you already know the answer to that question, but you'll be happy to know Kelly has no problem with you staying here for a few days over the holidays. The spare room is ready and waiting for you." It got quiet on Jackie's end, and I could almost hear the wheels spinning while she contemplated her next move.

"So, let me get this straight. You told her what we talked about the other day, and she still said it was okay for me to come?"

"Yes, that's right. It's that whole 'taking the marriage vows seriously' thing again. She trusts me. And she has every reason to trust me because you and I are a non-issue. She knows that, I know that, and deep down, you know it too, Jackie."

"That Kelly is a lucky girl." Jackie's volume was considerably louder than usual.

Kelly chuckled, rolled over on top of me, and nuzzled into the nape of my neck, employing a very effective distraction technique. "Beth's the lucky one!" She reached her hand under my shirt and began caressing my nipples. My ability to stay focused on the conversation with Jackie was dwindling, and my voice trailed off into a low moan.

"Are you two having sex right now?" Jackie asked, with a hint of both jealousy and annoyance.

"We will be as soon as you hang up." Kelly kissed me passionately and took the phone from my hand, putting it on the nightstand.

"Call me later, and we'll talk about your plans," I said, not caring if Jackie heard me or not. I was too focused on Kelly's lips, slowly making their way down my body, awakening the nerve endings along the way. In hindsight, I could see she was marking her territory. I belonged to Kelly, and she made sure I knew it. I was more than happy to oblige and let her claim me.

Chapter Three

I HELD THE LADDER while Kelly climbed high enough to reach the clips on the gutters that would hold our Christmas lights. I hated ladders and left all that kind of work on the house to her. Little did she know it was somewhat self-serving. Whenever a ladder was involved, I got to see her in her sexy work boots and a baseball cap. Today, it was her Atlanta Braves hat turned backward with her blond hair pulled back into a ponytail. She sported a loose-fitting T-shirt partially tucked into her jeans, and I had to restrain myself from taking her right there on the winter-browned front lawn. The neighbors probably wouldn't appreciate that move, so I controlled myself.

It was a typical December day in Atlanta, which was a pretty vague description of the weather, considering there is no typical day in December in Atlanta. It's either seventy-five degrees or twenty degrees, or anywhere in between. Today, thank goodness, it was T-shirt warm. A balmy seventy-two without a cloud in the sky—perfect for outdoor decorating. As she worked up on the ladder, I positioned myself with an excellent view of her breasts underneath her shirt. If I was going to be bored just standing there and holding the ladder, you could bet I was going to amuse myself.

I snapped out of my daydream of fornicating on the grass with my wife when a black BMW convertible pulled into our driveway. Jackie Fairburn peered at us over the tops of her Ray-Bans and flashed her typical confident smile. I looked up at Kelly and found her glancing back at Jackie with her best 'bring it on' expression. Kelly's confidence was one of her sexiest characteristics. I love a woman who knows who she is and the power she possesses, and Kelly knows both. If Jackie came to play, she'd best be prepared for a formidable opponent. Kelly climbed down the ladder, and we walked to the car to help Jackie with her Louis Vuitton luggage.

"Hey, girls! The house looks great. I can't wait to see those lights once it gets dark tonight. You do good work, Kelly. And Beth, nice job holding that ladder."

"Gee, thanks, smart ass. Good to see you, too." I leaned in and hugged her, recognizing the familiar scent of her hair products. She'd aged a bit, but then again, who hadn't? But she still had those killer green eyes I used to get lost in when we were dating. I flattered myself that her fresh-from-the-salon shoulder-length brown curly hair was styled precisely as she knew I would like it. "Nice car. The business must be doing pretty well, huh?"

"It's growing nicely, thank you." She reached over and gave Kelly a firm hug, which I noticed was only half-heartedly returned by my wife. "Thanks for letting me stay, Kel. I appreciate it. I hate hotels, and I sure as hell didn't want to stay with my mom."

Kelly gave me a sideways glance and mouthed, 'Kel?' when Jackie turned her back. I shrugged my shoulders in response.

"It's no problem. We're happy to have you. Come in, and let's get you settled in the guest room."

Kelly and Jackie grabbed the suitcases, which I noticed were large enough to make me wonder exactly how long she was planning to stay. As we walked toward the front door, the dogs sat patiently, waiting to greet their guest.

"Hey, guys!" Jackie said enthusiastically as I opened the door, and they came rushing out to tackle her. Any friend of ours was a friend of our dogs, so they made sure to give Jackie special guest treatment.

"Okay, Oliver. Leave Aunt Jackie alone. Jake! She does not want your cold nose in her face!" I tried unsuccessfully to pull them away from her.

"It's okay. I love it. I've been thinking about getting a dog of my own. My cat is cute, but I don't get a greeting like this when I come home."

"That's true, but I would think your lifestyle might not be suitable for a dog. They sort of demand that you be home more often than not. That's not really your M.O., is it, Jackie?" I asked, with more than a little passive-aggressive intent in my voice.

She glared at me in response as if to scold me for my implication. "Well, the new me plans to be home a lot. I told you—I'm turning over a new leaf."

"Forgive me for being skeptical," I said.

"That's okay. You don't have to believe me. The truth is, I've reached a point in my life where I want what you have. Actually, I want *you*, but your wife seems reluctant to let that happen." She shot a sideways glance at Kelly. It was obvious the gloves were coming off quickly.

Kelly looked a bit shocked, but she smiled. "Wow. You didn't take long to come out with *that*, did you? I admire your boldness. You've got some big balls; I'll give you that."

I was equally shocked but held it in check. "Uh, excuse me.

What makes you think it's just Kelly keeping this from happening? Jackie, don't make us regret the invitation for you to stay. You are not starting off on the right foot."

Jackie put both hands up in a *mea culpa* manner. "Relax, relax. I was just making a joke. Geez, have you guys lost your sense of humor? I'm sorry. Touchy subject, I guess. I promise not to break up your marriage while I'm here." She put her index and middle finger up on her right hand. "Scout's honor."

"Seriously, Jackie. If you want to turn over a new leaf, I'm all in favor, but I know you too well. You can't resist any hot girl who crosses your path. It will take an awfully strong woman to deal with your wandering eye. A better woman than I, that's for sure, since we both know I couldn't handle it."

Kelly chimed in to dial down the tension in the room. "Hey, I have an idea. How about we save the heavy conversations for later when we all have a glass of wine in our hands, shall we? We went from zero to a hundred as soon as you walked in the door."

"Fair enough, babe," I said, making a mental note to thank Kelly later for extricating us from that conversation.

We left Jackie in the guest room for a bit, allowing her to unpack and settle in. In the meantime, we went back outside to finish the Christmas lights. I could see Kelly's wheels were spinning, but I thought it might be wise to let her be. She'd say something when she was ready, and until then, I played the dutiful and helpful wife.

We agreed to order a pizza and maybe catch a movie on Netflix after dinner. It would provide a welcome distraction from any further discussion. I did not want to referee a sparring contest between Kelly and Jackie. Something told me the ref would be the one to get TKO'd in that match-up.

* * * *

We all behaved during dinner, getting caught up on this and that. Jackie told us about her recent break-up, admitting that it was precipitated by her cheating with a woman she met at a bar. I tried not to express my lack of surprise, but I'm sure she saw right through me. She seemed genuinely sad that this affair had ended and confessed that she was aware of her penchant for sabotaging relationships. It seemed like a step toward inner growth, but it was also too small of a sample size to draw any conclusions as to her maturity.

Later that night, Kelly was unusually silent while lying in bed with me, snuggled into the crook of my arm. I stroked the hair off her forehead, trying to gauge whether she wanted to talk, sleep, or fool around. Kelly was easy to read if she was talking. It's when she goes quiet that I start to worry. I made a sound of contentment while stroking her arm, hoping she would clue me in as to her mood.

"You feel extra warm tonight, babe. Are you feeling all right? We could turn the heat off in this room, and I still wouldn't need a blanket."

"I'm fine. I'm just snuggled and cozy, so I guess I'm radiating. Want me to move off you?"

"Oh, hell no. I want you to move *on* me, but I can't tell if you're in the mood or not. Is Jackie's presence here upsetting you?"

"No. I feel sorry for her. If she got her shit together, she'd probably make a good partner for someone. She's smart, successful, and beautiful, but to be clear, that partner is *not* you." I could feel her cheeks move as they pressed against my chest, indicating she was smiling.

"I don't want her. You know that. There's only one woman I want, and I've already found her. She's burrowing her head into my neck as we speak, but yes, you're right. Deep down, Jackie is a good person. She just has serious commitment issues, and she can't be faithful."

"Just? You make it sound like those are trivial things."

"If I thought they were trivial, I wouldn't have broken up with her all those years ago."

"I don't think I've ever asked you this. Was she any good in bed?"

I froze, knowing it was a trick question. No answer would keep me out of trouble. I'd be lying if I said no, and she would see right through me. If I said yes, she'd want to know more. No good could come from this conversation.

"You don't really want me to answer that, do you?"

She laughed, raised her head off my chest, and leaned on her elbow. "What you really mean to say is that you don't *want* to answer that. Am I right?"

"Can't I just plead the fifth?"

"No. I'm a big girl. What's the answer to the question, Beth?"

I sighed, realizing there was no way out. "Yes, she was good in bed. There, are you satisfied?"

"Not really. Somehow, I knew that was going to be the answer.

She couldn't get *that many* women to sleep with her if she was no good in bed. I figured she must have some sexual superpower."

"That's a bit extreme, don't you think?"

"Well, you stayed with her for two years even though she cheated. There had to be something keeping you there."

"I thought she would mature. And change. I guess I thought I could be the one to change her, but we all know that's not what happened."

"Was she better than me?" Kelly looked me in the eye, waiting to see if I would hesitate in my response. I didn't.

"No. Definitely not. No one is better than you."

"Are you just saying that to keep yourself out of trouble?"

"No. I've never been more satisfied in bed than I am with you. It's like you know exactly where and how to touch me. Now *that's* a superpower." I rolled over on her, kissing her neck and fondling her breasts.

"I see I've done it again. I got you all hot and bothered while talking about sex with another woman." She ruffled her fingers through my hair.

"No, you got me hot and bothered talking about sex with you. So can we please stop talking and let me have my way with you?"

"You'll have to be quiet. We don't want Jackie to hear us. Knowing her, she'll come through that door and try to join in."

"Maybe I should lock it," I said, getting up and doing just that. It seemed highly unlikely that Jackie would barge in looking for a menage, but better safe than sorry.

As I returned to the bed, I crawled under the covers at the foot of the bed and worked my way up, kissing Kelly's legs and parting them to take my place in her warmth. I wasn't lying to her when I said she's the best I've ever had. As I put my head between her legs and breathed her in, I was overcome with a sense of euphoria.

Kelly ran her fingers through my hair and moaned, making me want to find that place in her that made her lose all control. She squirmed as I made my way to that spot, and once I found it, I stayed focused on her pleasure. The release from her body to mine was like an electrical current, coursing through my nerve endings until I joined her in orgasmic ecstasy. She breathed heavily as I made my way up to kiss her, the taste of her fresh on my lips. I rolled onto my back and pulled her into me, needing to feel her heart beating with mine while I caught my breath. I wiped the perspiration from her forehead and kissed her while she recovered from the aftershocks.

As she fell asleep in my arms a few minutes later, I whispered in her ear, being careful not to wake her.

"Only you can do this to me, my love. Only you."

Chapter Four

KELLY WAS STILL ASLEEP when I woke the following day, so I threw on sweatpants and my favorite long-sleeved T-shirt and took the dogs out of the bedroom so she could sleep in. On the way down to the kitchen, I smelled the intoxicating aroma of brewing coffee. Jackie had made herself at home already, which I was grateful for in this instance because it meant hot coffee was waiting for me. I poured myself a tall mug full, opened the back door to let Oliver and Jake out, and found Jackie sitting on the patio in a lounge chair, a blanket over her shoulder and a steaming beverage in her hand.

"Good morning. You're up early." I sat in the chair next to hers.

"Yeah, I woke up around six and my brain kicked in immediately, so going back to sleep was impossible."

"Did you sleep well?"

"Eventually. Once the noise from the bedroom down the hall subsided," she said with a wink and a wry smile.

"Yeah...sorry about that."

"No, you're not, but that's okay. I can't say I blame you. It sounded like someone had a *very* enjoyable experience." I blushed and hid my face behind my coffee cup. "Is she better than me?"

"Why does everyone keep asking me that? Kelly wanted to know the same thing about you last night."

"And?"

"When you find the one you're supposed to be with forever, that's the best. I don't know how else to answer the question without being disingenuous or hurtful."

"So that's a fancy way of saying yes, she's better than me."

"She's better *for* me. Yes." I wrapped my fingers around the warm mug and took another sip of coffee.

"I'm happy for you. And jealous. I admit it. I came here thinking I could just convince you that we should try again, but I was wrong."

"Would you really want to be with someone who would just leave the woman she's committed to?"

"It wouldn't be the first time I convinced a woman to cheat or to break a vow."

"Time to grow up, Jackie. You aren't going to find something real until you realize women who will sleep with you without regard for the sanctity of their relationship will not make good long-term partners."

"Sanctity, huh? That's an awfully impressive word for seven o'clock in the morning. Do you always wake up dripping with wisdom before you've even had a full cup of coffee?"

"You're deflecting, Jack."

"I know. You think I'm not self-aware, but you're mistaken. In fact, I'm overly aware. And that's why I'm here, I guess."

"What do you mean?" I asked.

"I think I needed to come face to face with both the mistakes I've made and the vision of what I'm trying to find. Both of those realizations are right here in this house."

I gave that some thought. She had obviously done some soul-searching, and I didn't want to discourage that, but I also didn't want to be the primary focus of her introspection. She probably needed to figure that all out *without* me and my relationship in the middle of it all.

"So, am I like the Ghost of Christmas Past? Seeing what you messed up a decade ago? Or is it the Ghost of the Future, getting a glimpse of what you could have had if you'd done things differently?"

She smiled and said, "You always did have a way of getting to the heart of the matter. I must admit, I miss that."

"Does that mean I'm right?"

"I hadn't thought of it like that, but yeah—I guess you're right on both counts. The question is, what do I do about it? It's not enough to say out loud that I know what I want. Somehow, I have to unlearn all that stupid shit I've been doing my entire adult life. Because if I don't, nothing is going to change."

"Have you thought about therapy?" I asked.

"Yes, I've considered it. I guess I need someone to call me out on my bullshit. I guess maybe I thought that someone would be you."

"Well, much as I enjoy calling you out on bullshit, I'm not sure I'm qualified for the job. With all due respect, Jack...you've got a lot of baggage that needs to be unpacked. You need someone who can help you understand where your insecurities come from and why you feel the need to sleep with every woman in town to overcompensate."

She cringed. "Ouch. I think you underestimate your ability to cut through my crap. You're doing an excellent job of it."

I immediately regretted my direct approach. "I'm sorry. I didn't mean to be hurtful. You know me—I say what's on my mind, for better or worse. I apologize."

"You don't have to apologize for being right." She stared off into the trees behind our house, clearly not looking at the scenery. The back door opened, and Kelly came out in her robe and slippers. The dogs rushed over to say good morning to her. She spent about five minutes cooing over them and came to me for a quick peck on the cheek.

"When did the dogs start getting more attention than me?" I asked, with a pouty look on my face.

"I think that happened the day we got the dogs," she replied. "You two look like you are in a heavy-duty conversation. Shall I go back inside and leave you to it?"

Jackie chimed in first. "No, it's nothing you can't hear. Your wife was giving me her brutally honest opinions about the current state of my life."

"Did you expect otherwise, Jackie? You should know by now that Beth doesn't pull any punches. You either get brutally honest, or you get silence. She doesn't know how to communicate any other way."

"I know. Maybe that's why I'm here. I needed some tough love."

"Well then, you're in the right place." She turned to look at me. "Oh babe, before I forget. I got a text from my sister this morning. She'll be here tomorrow around noon-ish."

Jackie turned to me with a look of concern. "You didn't tell me you were having other guests. Now I feel bad that I'm intruding on a family thing."

"Don't worry about it," I said. "Her sister, Paige, also planned a bit of a last-minute holiday trip. She's fun, and you'll like her. We have plenty of room, so there was no reason to put either of you off."

"Is she straight?" Jackie asked jokingly, knowing the question would get an immediate reaction.

Kelly went red in the face and did a poor job of withholding her reaction. "Jackie! You are *not* to hit on her. Do you hear me?"

Jackie laughed. "Relax! I was just kidding. I promise." For the second time in two days, she put up the 'scout's honor' symbol with her two fingers. "But seriously, is she straight?"

Kelly closed her eyes, took a deep breath, and said, "As much as I know I'm going to regret saying this...no, she's not."

"You don't need to worry, Kelly. I won't let you down. I really am trying to be a better person. I know you won't believe me until you see it in action, but that's okay. I get it."

Jackie stood, picked up her empty cup, and went inside, with Oliver and Jake on her heels. Kelly came over and sat on my lap, her arms around my neck. She kissed me softly with her coffee lips, and I made a guttural sound of enjoyment. I put my hands low on her back and pulled her into me, nuzzling her neck.

"You left me early this morning," she said. "I rolled over hoping to grab a quickie before we started the day, only to realize I was cold and alone."

"Cold? Really?"

"Okay, not cold, but definitely alone."

"She heard us making love last night," I said with a grin that was half embarrassment and half pride.

Kelly immediately blushed. "She did? Oh, god. I'm so embarrassed. I thought I was being quiet."

"Babe, you are never quiet, and I love that about you."

"What did she say?"

"She said it sounded like you were having a very enjoyable time."

"Well, that's an understatement. Why do you think I woke up horny again this morning? Geez, I can't even face her now!"

I laughed and put my hands on her cheeks, pulling her close for a kiss. "You are adorable, you know that? Relax. She's fine. Oh, and just like you, she asked me if you were better in bed than she was. I said, 'why does everyone keep asking me that?'"

"And what was your response?"

"The same response I gave you last night. Yes, you are better."

"How did she take that news?"

"She said she's happy for me, and she's jealous. I think she is trying to change. We'll find out as soon as the next pretty girl comes along." I thought about mentioning Kelly's sister in the same breath, but thought better of it. It didn't matter, though. I know she was thinking about it just as I was.

Chapter Five

IN TYPICAL ATLANTA FASHION, Christmas Eve was about forty degrees colder than the previous days, so I was kneeling on the floor, ready to build a fire, when the doorbell rang. Kelly trotted down the stairs excitedly, anxious to see her little sister. They shrieked like schoolgirls while hugging as if they hadn't seen each other in decades instead of the three months that had passed since their last visit.

At the other end of the hallway, I saw Jackie from the corner of my eye. Knowing her as well as I did, I could see she was holding back in an effort to keep her promise to Kelly. I stepped in and took my turn, giving Paige an enveloping bear hug. She looked so much like Kelly it was almost unnerving. They were Irish twins, only eleven months apart, with Paige being the younger of the two. She had the same bright blue eyes I loved so much in Kelly, but her smile was just a bit different, making it the only real distinction between them.

I used to tell Kelly I thought her sister had a touch of sadness in her smile—if such a thing was possible in what should otherwise be a happy facial expression. Only a handful of family and friends knew why the sad smile was well-earned. When she was eighteen, she and her girlfriend Lori were an adorable young baby dyke couple, madly in love. Paige was planning their future, picking colleges where she knew they would both be accepted.

A few weeks before their freshman term began, Lori was meeting Paige to look at an off-campus apartment near Georgia Tech. She stepped off the curb to cross the street when a van swerved to avoid a cat crossing the road. It plowed onto the sidewalk, hitting Lori head-on, instantly killing her and seriously wounding several others. Paige was already in the building, viewing the apartment on the third floor, and she heard the screeching tires. She looked out the window to find her future lying lifelessly on the pavement. That sadness in her smile was well-earned.

Jackie patiently waited to be introduced, keeping her eyes above Paige's neck, clearly resisting the urge to take her in from head to toe. I was impressed at her self-control and made a mental note to commend her for good behavior when the time was right.

"Paige, meet Jackie. Jackie, this is Paige. Jackie is an old friend of ours, and she also happens to be Beth's ex-girlfriend."

"Hey, Jackie. Nice to meet you." Paige extended her hand,

which Jackie held on to just a second longer than necessary. The gesture was reciprocated, and they locked eyes for an instant, causing Kelly to step in to break it up.

"Paige, the dogs are patiently waiting for you to acknowledge them." Kelly grabbed her arm and pulled her toward Jake and Oliver. They whimpered with excitement as she bent down to pet them. I looked at Jackie and gave her a 'don't you dare' scowl. She mouthed the words 'I know' several times before turning away from me to avoid further scolding. This was not going to be easy.

Paige and Kelly were in the kitchen preparing Christmas Eve dinner while Jackie and I sat in the living room watching a football game. I could hear them singing and laughing as they cooked in the other room, and it warmed my heart, for Kelly's sake. She worried about her sister a lot and had almost literally picked her up off the floor to help her get through the grief from Lori's death. It had taken years to get to the point where Paige could even say Lori's name without bursting into hysterics.

Kelly made it her personal mission in life to help Paige deal with the loss in a healthy way rather than sinking into depression and self-destructive behavior. To her credit, Paige spent years in therapy to get herself right again. I admired her tenacity because, in a similar situation, I'm not sure I could have done it. If I lost Kelly like that, I'm pretty sure I would have crawled into a hole and let myself disintegrate.

Jackie got up from the sofa with her empty beer bottle and went to the refrigerator for another. Paige tossed the salad on the island and immediately stopped talking when Jackie walked in.

"Well, don't let me interrupt, ladies. Please don't stop the conversation on my account. It sounded like you were just getting to the good part."

Paige looked at Kelly, her face turning about three shades of red. "It's nothing, really. We were just being silly."

"Must be either really funny or really embarrassing to make you blush like that. It's adorable, by the way. Do you care to share, or should I leave you to your sisterly hijinks?"

Paige looked at Kelly as if asking permission to let Jackie in on their little secret. Kelly shrugged. "Well, go ahead. I know you, Paige. You will eventually say it anyway, much to my dismay."

"Okay. If you must know, I was telling Kelly that you have a really adorable ass."

Jackie hemmed and hawed like a teenage boy trying to get the nerve to speak to the prom queen. "I...err, um...you think I have...really?"

"Really. And my sister seems hell-bent on convincing me your ass is not, in fact, adorable."

"Ah, that makes sense. Kelly, I'm surprised you aren't ushering me right out the front door to keep me from participating in this conversation."

Paige looked confused. "Why would she do that?"

"Because I don't think your sister wants me to flirt with you in response to that comment. You see, I have a bit of a reputation, and not in a good way. My track record with women is less than stellar, so I can't really blame her."

Kelly looked at Paige, trying to justify herself. "What? I refuse to apologize for protecting my baby sister. Jackie knows I love her, and I'm not judging. What she does with her life is her business, but yeah...I would rather she not focus her attention on you. So, sue me."

"There's just one problem with that explanation, Kel. It was me focusing on Jackie, not the other way around. It seems to me Jackie is not the problem here."

"I didn't say we had a problem. I was simply pointing out that perhaps you're mistaken, and Jackie's ass is *not* adorable." She laughed at herself, and Paige and Jackie joined in. I had been listening to this conversation from where I sat in the living room but never let my eyes veer from the television for fear of getting pulled into it by Kelly. I knew I would get an earful later that evening when we were alone, and I thought it best to stay out of it until then, but my plan was quickly thwarted.

"Hey, babe? Are you hearing this? I think you need to weigh in on this conversation," Kelly said.

"I think I would rather stick needles in my eyeballs. Can't I just stay over here and pretend to watch this game?"

"I'm afraid not. If I have to talk about your ex-girlfriend's ass, you do too."

I got up from the sofa and joined them in the kitchen. "What exactly is it that you would like my opinion on? Whether Jackie's ass is adorable or whether it's wise for Paige to be noticing Jackie's ass?"

"Can we please stop talking about my ass like it's an entity unto itself?" Jackie asked emphatically.

I agreed, mostly so I could get myself out of this discussion. "Yes, let's pretend we never had this conversation, shall we?"

Paige chimed in. "Okay, okay. It's my fault. Jackie, I'm sorry for objectifying your ass. And Kelly, I'm sorry I find it adorable. There. Is everyone okay now? Can we please just have dinner?"

"Yes, everything is ready. Beth, will you help me bring the dishes into the dining room, please?" Kelly picked up the platters and went into the other room. From the corner of my eye, I saw Paige walk behind Jackie and whisper something in her ear, eliciting a flirtatious giggle from Jackie. Something told me the attempt to keep these two apart was about to fail miserably.

At dinner, the conversation turned to less flirtatious banter. Paige told us about her latest job as a personal assistant to a highly successful music producer. And while the heavy metal genre of music wasn't necessarily to her taste, she enjoyed meeting the artists and spending time in the studio while her boss worked.

"I'll bet there aren't too many lesbians in the heavy metal world, right? It makes it hard to meet people at work that you can connect with," Jackie said.

"You're right about that. I think I've met one lesbian in the nine months I've been working with Ronnie, and she was kind of scary. What I wouldn't give for a singer-songwriter. Give me a girl with a guitar any day, please. While you're at it, put her up on stage in a pair of well-worn Levi's and her best Chuck Taylor's, and I'd be in heaven."

Jackie grinned and said, "I play guitar, you know." Kelly shot a look at Jackie across the table. I guess she didn't want to add anything to the list of things that Paige might like about Jackie.

"Oh really?" Paige asked, showing increased interest. "What kind of music do you play? Are you in a band?"

"No band. I just play for fun. Mostly the singer-songwriter stuff that you mentioned. I love James Taylor, Joni Mitchell, Sheryl Crow, Indigo Girls."

"Seems like it's a requirement for every lesbian with a guitar to love the Indigo Girls."

"Yeah, that's true. It's a cliché, but I love it all the same."

"I'd love to hear you play sometime. Do you have your guitar here?"

"No, I didn't think Beth and Kelly would be interested in hearing me play, so I left it at home."

"Thank god," Kelly said.

"That's too bad. It might have been fun—Christmas carols by the fire. Oh, well. You'll have to play for me someday."

"You realize Jackie seduced almost all her ex-girlfriends with that guitar, right? It's a major prop in her playbook."

"Does it work?" Paige asked, with a devilish grin on her face.

"Once again, your sister is trying her best to make me look bad, but that being said...yes, it works." Jackie's smile was ear to ear at this point, clearly undaunted by Kelly's attempts at sabotage.

After dinner, we sat in the living room and watched *It's a Wonderful Life*; required viewing in our house at Christmas. I snuggled with Kelly while Paige watched the movie, and Jackie fiddled with her phone. Movies from the 1940s were not her cup of tea, but to her credit, she stayed to keep us company. Kelly was getting annoyed with me nibbling on her ear while she was trying to pay attention. I got a blanket and threw it over us so I could let my hands wander, and I tried my best to get her going, knowing she couldn't let on that she was being fondled. She squirmed a little but kept her composure even though my hands were in her pants.

Jackie suddenly swung her legs off the ottoman and turned to Paige. "I'm going out for some air. Care to join me? I think these two might need a moment alone." She smiled, looking at me to let me know the cat was out of the bag, no pun intended.

"Sure. It is getting a little warm in here now that you mention it." Paige threw us both a look of acknowledgment. Jackie grabbed the dogs' leashes, causing an excited doggie-ruckus as they made their way out the door.

"Maybe giving them a reason to leave wasn't the best idea. The last thing we want is for them to spend too much time alone together," I said.

She pulled me closer and nibbled on my neck while grinding her hips into me. "Maybe we can worry about them later? In the meantime, you got me started, so can you finish the job, please? Five minutes ought to do it."

"Five minutes? Really?"

"Yeah, I'm halfway there already. You just need to push me over the edge."

Dutiful wife that I am, I pulled the blanket over my head and granted her request.

PAIGE AND JACKIE SLOWLY made their way around the neighborhood, letting Jake and Oliver sniff every blade of grass along the way. After some small talk about the weather, Jackie turned to more interesting conversation.

"Thanks for coming out with me. I needed a break. I love your sister and Beth, but damn...sometimes it's hard to be around them. They are the poster children for the perfect relationship."

"I know, but it's not all perfect. They work at it—a lot. I usually talk to my sister about once a week, and I can tell when they are going through a rough patch. It doesn't happen often, but it does happen. And when it does, neither one of them lets it fester. No conversation is off-limits. I admire them for their honesty. If I'm lucky, maybe someday I'll get the chance to have what they have again."

Jackie slowed her pace and looked at Paige. "Again?"

Paige looked away, realizing she had inadvertently opened the door to a topic that was not one she wanted to revisit. Jackie picked up on her hesitancy and immediately backtracked. "Hey, sorry. I wasn't trying to pry. I can tell by the look on your face you'd rather avoid whatever memory just flashed in front of your eyes." Jackie resumed her walking pace, letting Paige know she wasn't waiting for any further response on the subject, but Paige stood stock still on the sidewalk, her gaze focused toward the streetlight, although it was evident her mind was elsewhere.

Jackie walked back toward Paige. "Hey. Are you okay? If you want to talk about it, I've been told I'm a good listener."

"No, but thanks, though. I just got lost in a memory for a second. I'm back now." She gently tugged on Jake's leash to tear him away from whatever scent he was focused on in the bushes. "Anyway, as I was saying...someday, I want to grow up to be just like my sister."

"Yeah, she's probably a pretty good choice for your role model, but then again, your sister doesn't really like me, so it keeps me from getting to know her as much as I'd like."

"So, what's the deal? Why doesn't she like you? Is it because you used to date Beth?" Paige asked, stopping again to wait for Jake to take care of his important business. Jackie made her way across the street to a neighborhood children's playground. She tied Oliver's leash to a tree and sat down on one end of a seesaw, waiting for Paige to catch up.

"No, it's not really about Beth. That probably doesn't help the relationship, but it's not the root of the problem. To be fair, I've managed to tarnish my reputation with her—not to mention a few other people—by my own actions. Let's just say I haven't been," she raised her hands to demonstrate air quotes, "the best version of me that I could be up to this point in my life. I'm working on it, but I'm not there yet. Not by a long shot."

Paige attached Jake's leash to a tree next to Oliver and planted herself on the other end of the seesaw, balancing it to the center. They teetered and tottered without giving it much thought since that's what one does when seated on a seesaw.

"That's a rather vague assessment. Is that your way of getting me to mind my own business, or would you care to elaborate?"

"We'll freeze to death by the time we cover that subject in detail. There's a lot there. I was saving you from a long conversation in the cold."

"Well, first of all, I live in New York, so this is *not* cold. You southerners have no tolerance for anything below fifty degrees. It's downright balmy out here. Secondly, I'm also a good listener, so I'm returning the favor and offering an ear to chew on."

Jackie smiled. "Well, the old me would make a flirtatious joke about my desire to nibble on your ear. The new me is trying to learn not to say those things out loud."

Paige immediately blushed, smiled, and lowered her head, unsure how to respond to the remark. Jackie stopped the seesaw and smiled back, trying to decide where to go with this conversation. "I'm sorry. Now you see why your sister doesn't like me," she said.

"My sister is overprotective of me. I think I'm old enough to take care of myself when it comes to some flirty banter."

"Yeah, but the problem is she knows I don't stop at the banter. To say that I've had my share of dalliances that started with banter and ended up in bed would be the understatement of the decade."

"Well, were they all consensual dalliances?"

"Of course. I may sleep around, but I do have some principles. No means no. If a woman doesn't want me, then I wish her well and move on."

"So, then what is my sister's objection?"

"On more than one occasion—including in my relationship with Beth—I have failed the monogamy test. I always *think* I want to be faithful and stay with just one woman for a while, but inevitably, my eye wanders, and I sabotage it. I've lectured myself a hundred times to avoid anything that resembles a 'relationship,' but there's a part of me that really wants that, so I think I can commit. So far, I've never been able to do it. I always end up cheating. And that is why your sister doesn't want me anywhere near you."

Paige resumed the teetering and smiled. "Oh, I get it. She thinks I'm going to fall hopelessly in love with you, only to have you dump me after the first roll in the hay?"

"Well, I'm not sure that's…"

"Her hypotheses—and yours, to some extent—assumes that A) I'm going to want to sleep with you, B) that I'm going to fall in love with you, C) that you are going to dump me, and D) that I will be devastated if you do. That's a lot of assumptions, don't you think? My sister still thinks I'm the fragile eighteen-year-old who fell apart from her first broken heart. A lot of years have passed since I was that person."

"For the record, I never assumed you would want to sleep with me," Jackie said sheepishly. "I'm not quite that arrogant. Close, but not quite."

"I didn't think you were. I'm just giving you a hard time. You kind of set yourself up for that," Paige smiled as she abruptly exited the seesaw, causing Jackie to drop to the ground with a resounding thud.

"Damn. Your sister does *not* need to protect you. You've got that covered all by yourself. Consider me appropriately put in my place—literally and figuratively." Jackie faked an injury to her heart by putting both hands on the left side of her chest while she playfully rolled off the seesaw and onto the sand.

Paige walked over to her on the ground and lent her a hand to help her up. She pulled her with more effort than was required, which caused Jackie to spring up like a jack in the box and come to a halt within inches of Paige's face. They locked eyes for a second more than necessary before Paige stepped away and walked over to untie Oliver and Jake's leashes from the tree. She handed Oliver's leash to Jackie after she had brushed the sand off her Levi's, and they made their way back to the house without any further conversation.

Chapter Seven

KELLY AND I HAD long since finished our rendezvous on the sofa when I finally decided to express concern that Paige and Jackie had not yet returned from their walk. I didn't want Kelly to jump to conclusions, although I was pretty sure that in her head, she already had them rolling around behind a bush in the park while Jackie had her way with Paige. "So…it's been an hour. Should we send out a search party?"

Kelly took a deep breath before answering, confirming she was thinking exactly what I was thinking. "I knew Jackie couldn't keep her promise."

"Now, now. You don't know for sure that anything is happening. Let's give her the benefit of the doubt until we have reason to throw her out. Maybe they're just talking. Maybe Jake and Olly are being stubborn."

Kelly got up from the couch and went into the kitchen in a wordless 'I don't have anything nice to say, so I'm gonna keep my mouth shut' gesture. I heard the pantry door opening and the package of Oreos being opened.

Kelly doesn't stress eat often, but when she does, Oreos are always the *go-to* cookie. I silently hoped Jackie was prepared for the hornet's nest she would walk into when they got home. And right on cue, I heard the front door open as soon as the first cookie went into Kelly's mouth. She calmly finished chewing, took a sip of her tea, and met them in the foyer.

Kelly took the dog's leashes off and hung them by the door, still not acknowledging Paige and Jackie. They seemed to sense she was annoyed—in truth, they'd have to be blind *not* to sense it—so they started making small talk about wandering the neighborhood to see everyone's Christmas lights. Kelly was not buying it and made her feelings known.

"Hey, Jackie. You've got sand all over the back of your pants. Did you guys do it right in front of the jungle gym?"

Jackie was about to respond when Paige stopped her. "Kel, don't be ridiculous. You don't really think we were having sex, do you? The sand is from the seesaw. I dumped Jackie onto the ground when I got off of it. Believe me. If we were having sex, it would *not* be in the sand. I've done it. It's impossible to get sand out of those delicate lady parts, you know? And then it chafes and causes a rash. What a mess. It's just not worth it."

Jackie stood by, holding in a laugh, knowing if she cracked up at that moment, there would indeed be hell to pay. If I'm being honest, I was torn between laughing and golf-clapping at Paige for saying the perfect thing to pull the rug out from under Kelly's argument. She knew exactly how to diffuse her sister's anger and anxiety. I could see the air escaping from her lungs. And then, entirely unexpectedly, Kelly smiled at both of them. Not even a fake smile. No, this was an honest to goodness 'I concede. You've won this round' grin. I wanted to bow to Paige as the goddess of conflict diffusion and avoidance.

With that, Kelly put her arms around her sister, gave her a hug and a kiss, and said goodnight. Well done, Paige Gallagher. Well done.

Chapter Eight

MUCH LIKE THE PREVIOUS day, I met Jackie on the patio at seven in the morning, armed with a cup of coffee and a host of questions. She seemed only half awake when the dogs trotted over to lick her in the face. For a moment, that made me nervous because it was still relatively early when we called it a night, so she should be well-rested. I sent up a prayer to the universe that there hadn't been a midnight booty call down the hall and into Paige's bedroom.

"Good morning, sunshine. Why so sleepy? You look like you were up half the night. Please tell me you behaved yourself."

"Why does everyone think I'm going to seduce her? No, I stayed tucked away in my little room, keeping my hands to myself all night. I couldn't sleep, that's all. My brain refused to turn off."

"Penny for your thoughts?"

"What happened to Paige that makes Kelly so over-protective of her?"

"That's not my story to tell," I said, even though I would have liked to share it with her so she would understand what Paige had been through.

"We talked last night, and she got all squirrelly about her past at one point. I got the impression she was holding back something pretty painful."

"That's probably a fair statement, but it's not for me to say. It sounds like you two must have had some deep conversation. After all, it's not a topic that would generally come up in small talk. You were gone long enough to give Kelly a coronary, so…what happened?"

"We were getting to know each other, that's all. We talked about why Kelly doesn't like me and doesn't trust me. You needn't worry. I was honest about it and said Kelly has her legitimate reasons, but Paige is a tough cookie. She put me in my place—and Kelly, too, for that matter."

"Yeah, Kelly still thinks of her as her baby sister who needs protection when the truth is, Paige is probably stronger than all of us."

"I can see that. She impressed me."

"Yeah, well, don't let her impress you too much. She's still off-limits to you, okay? You promised Kelly."

"I know, I know, but between you and me, I find her very intriguing. She's someone I'd like to get to know better, even as just a friend."

"You are not capable of having attractive women as friends, Jack. Please don't tell Kelly you find her intriguing."

"I'm friends with you, aren't I?"

"Aww. That's very flattering, but we're only friends because *I* decided to stay in a friendly relationship with you after *you* cheated on me. And correct me if I'm wrong, but didn't you come here this week to get me to leave my wife for you? I think I've made my point."

"Okay, maybe you're right. So let me rephrase my thought. I want to *learn* how to become the kind of person who can be just friends with a woman. I may not be there yet, but I think I can grow into that person. I really want to. I'm too old for just sex. I need friends. I need a real relationship built on something other than how good she is in bed."

I looked at Jackie and was honestly shocked to find that she had tears in her eyes. I'd never once seen her cry about anything in the years I'd known her. She just didn't seem to have the emotional capacity to get to that depth of feeling. Maybe she was capable of change after all. I started feeling guilty for my lack of confidence in her.

* * * *

Paige and Kelly spent the day after Christmas shopping at the local crafts store for discounted holiday decorations. It was a tradition that started with their mother when they were little girls, and they maintained it to this day whenever they were together at Christmas. The plan was to meet Beth and Jackie for lunch, but Beth had called to say Jackie wasn't feeling well, so they bailed out.

Kelly suspected maybe Jackie was faking it because she didn't want to spend any unnecessary time with Kelly. After all, Kelly knew she wasn't being a very gracious hostess. If Paige wasn't there, she would probably have a very different attitude, but her desire to keep Jackie away from Paige took precedence over her need to be a good hostess.

At the restaurant, Kelly perused the menu while Paige got them a couple of drinks from the bar—iced tea for Kelly as the designated driver and vodka tonic for Paige. As the bartender poured the drinks, she gave Paige a far too obvious once-over. Paige wasn't sure if she should be flattered or offended, so she had a bewildered look on her face as she returned to the table.

"I think the bartender was hitting on me," she said.

Kelly whipped her head around to see the woman still looking at Paige with a big smile. "Well, that's rude. How does she know I'm not your girlfriend?"

"Probably because we look like twins, Kel. I think our sibling relationship is pretty obvious, don't you?" Paige glanced back toward the bar. "She's kind of cute, don't you think? At first, I was a little offended she was checking me out, but I'm blushing a bit, so I guess I'm not offended after all!"

"Yeah, well, don't get any ideas." Kelly turned her attention back to her menu. "You're not picking up some random bartender."

"Who said anything about picking her up? Kelly, seriously. You've got to stop acting like you need to protect me. I can take care of myself. I know you don't believe that, but it's true."

"I know you can. It's just everyone else that I don't trust."

"Let me ask you this. Do you think you would be this protective of me if Lori hadn't been killed?"

"That's hard to say. I'd like to think so, but I will admit watching you go through that has made me want to shield you from getting hurt again."

"Kelly, it was *sixteen* years ago. At some point, I *have to* start living my life. Lori would never have wanted me to spend decades mourning her. If the roles had been reversed, I would want her to be happy. To live a full life. I know she doesn't want me to be stuck like this forever."

"Am I contributing to your being 'stuck'?" Kelly asked, with a somewhat surprised look on her face.

"Not entirely, but to a small extent, yes. Let's take the incident last night, for example. I get that you don't like Jackie, and she told me why..."

"Oh, I'm sure she didn't give you half of why I don't want you to get involved with her." Kelly forcefully set her drink down on the table.

"I think you're wrong there. She admitted she'd been a pretty shitty person when it came to her relationships with women. She told me she sleeps around, can't be monogamous, and always screws things up. That's a pretty harsh assessment of herself, don't you think?"

"Let me tell you a story about Jackie. I will preface it by saying I don't dislike her. I think she's smart and funny, and she quite often amuses me. I just think she has no idea how to get out of her own way.

"When I first met Beth, and we were getting to the point where we were falling for each other, Beth met Jackie for dinner one night, for no other reason except Jackie was in town, and they hadn't seen each other in a while. They spent most of the dinner talking about Beth and me, how crazy she was about me, and how she thought I was going to be 'the one.' You know how it is at the beginning of a relationship when you're falling in love.

"Jackie sat at that table and told Beth how happy she was for her and how she couldn't wait to meet me, blah, blah, blah. And then, she started buying Beth drinks—lots of drinks. She got her shit-faced drunk, took her back to her hotel room, and slept with her.

"Beth woke up the next morning sick from the alcohol and sick with guilt. Jackie told her she must not be all that crazy about me if she could sleep with her ex at the drop of a hat. So that made Beth even more upset. She left Jackie's hotel room and came straight to my apartment, crying her eyes out. She told me what had happened and then she broke up with me. She said she was obviously a terrible person, and she needed to let me go so she wouldn't be able to hurt me again."

"Whoa," Paige said, looking completely shocked.

"Yeah. So now maybe you can see why I don't trust her." She reached for a piece of bread in the center of the table and angrily tore off a piece.

"So what happened? How did you get back together?"

"Well, aside from being devastated Beth had cheated on me, I was also furious. Even though I didn't know Jackie very well, I somehow knew in the back of my mind she seduced Beth on purpose to break us up, but what I couldn't understand was why. Why did she feel the need to sabotage us? Was it because if she couldn't have her, she didn't want anyone else to have her either? Or did she do it to prove to herself she could? Either way, it's a terrible thing to do.

"Anyway, Jackie was still in town for a few more days after that, but as far as I know, she didn't see Beth again. I figured she had accomplished what she wanted and was done with her. I spent that day after Beth left my apartment just heartbroken because, at that point in our relationship, I, too, thought Beth was 'the one,' and I was about to ask her to move in with me. I stayed in bed for the next two days, just wallowing in my pain. I called Beth a few times, but she wouldn't answer the phone. And then, at about midnight on the third day after she told me what had happened, my doorbell rang. I ran to the door, hoping it was Beth. As it turns out, it was Jackie. I didn't even know she knew where I lived. I was about to slam the door in her face, but she stuck her foot in the door and pleaded with me to let her in. So I did."

"Well, that takes balls, huh?" Paige said.

"Sure does, but that's Jackie. She had taken a taxi to my apartment because she was totally drunk. I asked her if she had just come from another alcohol-induced rendezvous with my girlfriend and was she happy now that she had broken us up. She said she hadn't seen Beth again, and in fact, she had come to apologize and to see if she could convince me to forgive Beth and take her back. So, of course, I said, 'why should I?' to which she responded, 'Because I've never seen Beth so in love with anyone else in all the years I've known her. And because you will miss out on something truly amazing if you don't.' And I'll be damned if she wasn't right.

"So if you recall, I started this conversation by saying it's not that I dislike Jackie. I do like her. She showed me a side of her that night that impressed me. She admitted she seduced Beth and got her too drunk to make the right decision about having sex with her. She took full responsibility. But when I say she can't get out of her own way, I mean that sincerely. She sabotages herself. She knew exactly what she was doing in that hotel room.

"I honestly believe she felt terrible about it when all was said and done. It's like she has this evil twin inside her that makes her do stupid, impulsive things. Most of the time, those things involve sleeping with women who either don't belong to her or aren't her girlfriend of the month. She says she wants to change and has grown up, but I'll believe it when I see it. I'm not convinced yet. So yes, I have good reason to ensure you don't get involved with her. I may like her, but I don't trust her for a second." She reached for the bread again, tearing off another piece as if it represented Jackie's head.

Paige took the last sip of her drink and signaled the bartender for another. "So, did you go see Beth that night to get back together?"

"No, I didn't. I was still so hurt she had cheated on me, so I was going to think it over for a while, but as it turns out, when Jackie left my apartment, she took the taxi to Beth's and told her the same thing— that she needed to find a way to get me to forgive her because I now knew the truth of what happened and it wasn't Beth's fault. An hour later, there was another knock on my door."

Chapter Nine

7 YEARS EARLIER

I PARKED THE CAR, ran into the building, and took the steps two at a time to get to Kelly's apartment. I was sweating and nervous but somehow found the courage to knock on the door. I figured when she saw me through the peephole, she'd go back to bed. After all, it was three in the morning, and I was sure she didn't want to talk to me. I couldn't blame her. I had betrayed her—plain and simple. She had no reason to forgive me. Why should she?

I tried to come up with at least one valid reason to plead my case when she opened the door. Her eyes were red and puffy, and she was wearing her old pajamas that looked like they had been through the washing machine ten million times. She had only one sock on, and her hair was sticking straight up in the back. And yet, she was still the most beautiful woman I had ever seen. I burst into tears the minute I saw her. She leaned her head against the door jamb while I bawled my eyes out in the hallway.

Kelly grabbed my hand and led me into her apartment. The place was a mess. Open Oreos and Cheetos bags were on the coffee table, along with assorted mugs and glasses of various beverages. It was evident Kelly's last couple of days were as miserable as mine. Since I knew I was the cause of all this pain, my feelings of guilt increased exponentially.

I sat on the chair next to her sofa, unsure where to begin. I guess Kelly could see that because she started the conversation for me.

"I saw Jackie," she said.

"I know. I did too. She told me she had been here. I'm sorry you had to deal with that."

"She said it was all her fault."

"Yeah, so I heard. But the thing is, I have to take some responsibility for what I did. I have to live with what I've done to you."

"How much of it do you remember?" she asked.

"Not much, if I'm being honest. I have a vague recollection of walking into her hotel room. There are snippets of stuff after that, but I can't recall much. To be clear, it's not like she raped me or anything. I want to make sure you know that. I was there. I participated. I am to blame. I want you to know how sorry I am for betraying you and the trust you had in me. I don't expect to be able to get that back again, and Kelly, I swear it's like a knife in my heart." I started crying again. Actually, I'm not sure I had ever stopped in the first place. It had been three solid days of tears, so I wasn't really keeping track of their ebb and flow.

Kelly went into the kitchen to get me a glass of water. Before handing it to me, she took my hand and led me to the sofa to sit next to her. I took a sip of the drink, which was nice and cold, and it felt good—like it started to cool the flaming angst I was feeling. She pulled my head close to her and rested it on her shoulder. My crying escalated, and I held on tight while my guilt spilled out all over her. To her credit, she just let me cry. She wasn't angry—well, not outwardly, at least. I thought I heard a few sobs coming from her, but it was probably just me, echoing in sadness.

After what seemed like an eternity, she finally spoke. "Where do we go from here?"

I looked at her incredulously. I thought that had already been decided, and we would go our separate ways. It never occurred to me she might forgive me. "What? I mean...I just assumed..."

"Assumed what? That we were through? Maybe we are, but don't you think we should at least talk about it? You ended it here the other day without giving me the chance to tell you how I felt."

"Because I don't deserve you, Kelly. Any woman who would do this to you is not good enough for you."

"I should have some say in that, don't you think?"

"I was trying to do the right thing after I had done the most wrong thing I could have ever done."

"I want you to tell me how it happened. All of it."

I looked up at her wide-eyed, trying to imagine why on earth she would possibly want to hear about how this happened. I was silently begging her to let me off the hook. "Kel, please. You don't want to hear this."

"Yes, I do."

"But why?"

"Because I need to know where the weakness is in our relationship. What caused you to cross that line."

"Well, mostly it was alcohol..."

"So I need to be worried whenever you have too much to drink?"

"No, I...it's not that...I just..."

"Tell me how it happened. Maybe the answer will reveal itself in the telling."

I sighed and gulped down the rest of the water. "Do you have anything other than water? I'm going to need something stronger."

Kelly got up and poured me a glass of whiskey. It wasn't my choice of drink, but it would have to do because, at that moment, I couldn't fathom how I would get through this. She handed it to me and I drank it in one shot, so she refilled it again. I decided to pace myself on the second glass. After all, alcohol had contributed to this mess in the first place.

* * * *

The Four Seasons Hotel restaurant was lovely, with soft music and the clinking of plates and glasses in the background. The aroma of garlic seemed to waft from every table, and I was so hungry it made me salivate. I asked the waiter for some bread while I waited for Jackie to join me. She was fashionably late as usual, which was ironic, considering her room was only an elevator ride from where I sat. Knowing Jackie, she wanted to make an entrance.

When she walked toward me, I had a flashback to a time when we were dating all those years ago. Our first official date was at an expensive restaurant, and she worked hard to impress me. She wore a black jacket over a green blouse, both of which had been tailored to perfection. The green matched her eyes, and I couldn't help but be captivated. And now, she seemed to be trying just as hard to impress me here at the Four Seasons, which confused me since she knew I was in a new relationship. I got up from my seat to hug her, and I noticed she was wearing the same cologne she knew I liked.

"You're looking well, as usual, Jackie." I hugged her.

"You're not looking so bad yourself. New love agrees with you."

I could feel myself blushing. Any mention of Kelly gave me a little thrill, so I was sure my face was beet red. "It *does* agree with me."

As we took our seats, she said, "So, tell me about her. Any woman who can put that look on your face must be pretty special."

"Well, I don't know about the look on my face, but I can confidently say she is indeed pretty special. She's a lawyer. She's funny and kind and much smarter than me, so I'm always on my toes. She's thoughtful, and she makes me want to be thoughtful right back because she deserves it. And it doesn't hurt that she's ridiculously attractive." I smiled as I said it.

"Sounds like you're madly in love. Am I right?"

"Yes. I think she may be the woman I'm going to spend the rest of my life with."

"Wow. That's big news. Are you going to ask her to marry you?"

"It's too soon for that, but I can see that happening somewhere down the road if all goes well."

Jackie signaled for the waiter, and I was ready to give him my order when she interrupted.

"I think we'll start with some drinks before dinner. We've got a lot of catching up to do. Bring us two bourbons, please." She dismissed the waiter before I could object.

"I'm starving, Jack. I haven't eaten since breakfast. Bourbon on an empty stomach is a recipe for disaster."

"Oh, come on. I haven't seen you in ages. Allow me to toast to your good fortune."

"Okay, but just one."

Famous last words. We did finally order our entrees, but not before Jackie had ordered three rounds of drinks. I could feel myself getting tipsy, but I figured I'd be fine as soon as some food hit my system.

We ate and talked for a long time, catching up on my job and her consulting business. We talked about women. Specifically, the long line of women Jackie had been with since we last spoke. She hadn't changed a bit since we broke up. It took me a while to notice that each time the subject of Kelly came up again, she would order another round of drinks. By the time dessert came, I could barely form complete sentences, so I had begged her to stop with the drinks and get me some coffee. In true Jackie form, she ordered me an Irish coffee with Baileys. At that point, I didn't have the wherewithal to object. I was feeling good, reminiscing about the past and going on and on about my future with Kelly.

By the time she paid the check, I was plastered, but somehow, Jackie was still completely in control, even though she had matched me drink for drink. She grabbed my hand to help me walk, my legs barely cooperating. I tried to articulate that I needed her to call me a taxi, but we were already in the elevator before the words finally came out.

I felt my stomach drop as the elevator whooshed up to the twenty-fifth-floor penthouse. I held on to her for dear life, trying hard not to fall over and not to vomit. I don't even remember getting into the room, but I do recall commenting on the sheer size of it and thinking Jackie's business was obviously thriving. I sat on the sofa, trying to figure out how I would get to the bathroom if and when my body decided to expel the dinner and drinks. I heard Jackie call down to the lobby to ask for an extra toothbrush, but I don't remember hearing the knock on the door when it was delivered.

I must have passed out briefly because when I looked up again, Jackie was sitting next to me, a glass of water in her hand. I declined it, but she insisted I would have one hell of a hangover if I didn't get some water in my system. She made me hold it with two hands, but I still managed to spill most of it onto my shirt. She got up to get a towel, but it was drenched, and I didn't object when I realized she was pulling my shirt over my head.

"Your tolerance for liquor has definitely diminished since we dated," she said.

"I hardly ever drink anymore since Kelly doesn't drink much."

"Do you ever stop thinking about Kelly?" she asked, with a hint of either jealousy or anger. "Maybe I can get you to focus on me for just a little while. You used to be pretty good at that, as I recall." She leaned closer to me.

"Are you trying to seduce me, Jackie?"

"I'm considering it. You are in my hotel room with no shirt on after all." She looked me in the eyes, and I got lost for a minute. I remember flashing back to the hundreds of times we'd had sex in the past. It almost always started with the look she was giving me at that moment.

Jackie reached over to brush a lock of hair off of my face. She leaned in to kiss me, but pulled back. I think she wanted to see if I would lean in too, and I did, much to my surprise. And I leaned in again when she moved toward me, kissing her softly. I suddenly felt very vulnerable, given that I was half-naked and Jackie was looking at me with pure lust in her eyes. She pulled me closer and kissed me again, her tongue tantalizing me. In the back of my mind, there was a half-conscious thought that I should pull away because this was wrong, but her kiss was so intoxicating that my body refused to take heed.

Jackie continued kissing me passionately as she reached around my back and undid the clasp of my bra, pulling it off and throwing it on the floor. I pulled her shirt over her head, and she pushed me down onto the couch, her hand guiding my breast into her mouth. I remembered how good it felt to feel her body on mine, even as the guilt of cheating on Kelly weighed heavily. She undid the button and zipper of my pants, expertly removing them and my underwear without a hint of clumsiness. As she guided my legs apart and put her tongue on me, all thoughts of Kelly vanished, and I lost myself in the throes of orgasmic ecstasy.

* * * *

I woke up at six in the morning after dreaming a jackhammer had entered my skull at the left temple and was drilling its way through my brain. When I opened my eyes, I realized that while the jackhammer itself was metaphoric, the pain it was inflicting was all too real.

The curtains were wide open, and the rising sun was streaming through the window like a laser beam straight into my eyeball. I lifted my head a couple of inches off the pillow and saw Jackie sitting in the chair, drinking coffee and scrolling through something on her cell phone. There was room service breakfast on the table, and the smell of it turned my stomach. You know you're having a bad morning when the smell of bacon makes you sick.

Jackie noticed I was awake, and she smiled at me. Her hair was wet, and she wore a bathrobe loosely tied at the waist, making it painfully clear the robe was the only thing covering her very naked body. I took a quick peek under the covers to see if I was equally as naked. I cringed.

"Good morning, sunshine," she said.

"There is not one good thing about this morning," I grunted. My voice was deep and gravelly. "Jackie, what did we do?"

She stood up, and what little coverage there was from the robe vanished as the waist belt fell by the wayside. As she walked toward me, I rolled over in the opposite direction to avoid the lady parts that were about to be just inches away from my face. I crawled out from the other side of the bed, pulling the sheet with me to cover myself.

Jackie sat down in the spot I had just vacated on the bed. "Beth, I'm hurt. Do you mean to tell me you don't remember anything about our passionate lovemaking?" she said with as much sarcasm as she could muster. "We had quite a nice little trip down memory lane once I finally got you to stop talking about Kelly. You've learned a few nice moves. I'm impressed."

Shit. Kelly. It suddenly clicked. I ran into the bathroom and vomited. When I was no longer in possession of the contents of my stomach, I grabbed the sink and pulled myself up. When I saw my face in the mirror, I burst into tears. Jackie obviously heard me bawling and knocked on the door.

"Let me in, Beth. Please?"

"No. Can you just bring me my clothes?" I said through the sobs. "I've got to get out of here. I need to see Kelly."

"You aren't going to be foolish enough to tell her about this, are you?"

"Of course I am. I can't keep this from her. If we don't have honesty, we don't have anything."

She knocked again and handed me my clothes. "I would argue that if you don't have fidelity, you don't have anything either. If she was your one and only true love, what are you doing here in my hotel room on the morning after having sex with me?"

"You got me drunk!" I was clumsily putting on my underwear.

"Yeah, but you were not unwilling. As I recall, there was more than one moment when you begged me to fuck you. Be honest with yourself, Beth. You were not here under duress."

"I'm sober now. This was a mistake, Jackie. A huge mistake. I have to go see her."

"It's six in the morning. She's probably not even awake yet. Take a few minutes to think about this before you say something you will regret."

"Jackie, forgive me, but you're not exactly the person to go to for successful relationship advice."

I leaned over the sink and splashed water on my face. I swished some water around in my mouth, then attempted to tame the nest of hair on top of my head, quickly realizing it was a lost cause. If there was such a thing as 'sex head,' I was undoubtedly modeling that style. I made sure I was all buttoned and zipped, and I opened the bathroom door.

Jackie was blocking my exit, and I nearly bumped into her as I tried to make my way out.

"Please get out of my way." I gently nudged her, and she put her arms on my shoulders and leaned in so her face was inches from mine. She leaned in to kiss me, and I started to cry again. I didn't kiss her back, but I didn't stop her either. She kissed the tears from my cheeks. I wanted so badly to pull away, but my need for consolation overwhelmed my good judgment at that moment. She kissed me again, and I reciprocated. Her hands moved from my face to my breasts and pressed against me. Something clicked in my brain. I stopped kissing her, stepped back, and walked around her.

"Goodbye, Jackie," I said, as I picked up my keys and left the hotel to confess my sins to Kelly.

Chapter Ten

"WHY DID YOU LET her kiss you—again? More importantly, why did you kiss her back?" Kelly asked, after I finished telling her what had happened with Jackie.

"I honestly have no idea. I asked myself that question all the way over here. I was so upset—so vulnerable. I needed to be consoled, I guess."

"That's interesting. I've consoled many crying people, and it never led to making out."

"I know. It's a terrible excuse. That's why I decided to break up with you." I started crying again and pulled a tissue out of the box. "Because it's inexcusable." I could barely get the words out through my tears. I looked over at Kelly and was surprised to see she was crying too, which made me even more upset. To be the source of all this pain was killing me.

I looked down at my hands and noticed the bracelet Kelly had given me for Christmas. I nervously twirled it in my fingers, eventually grasping the clasp and taking it off. I moved onto the couch next to Kelly and placed it in the palm of her hand.

"I'm so sorry, Kelly. You are the best thing that has ever happened in my life, and I've foolishly and recklessly thrown it away. I fell in love with you the minute I met you, and I will love you until the day I die. I hope you find someone who treats you better than I did." I took her hand and kissed it, then set it back on her lap and got up to leave.

"Where are you going?" she asked indignantly.

"I'm leaving."

"You're not even going to *try* to fight for me?"

I stopped in my tracks, unsure of what to do. My shoulders shuddered as my crying increased yet again. Kelly stood up and walked over to me. She handed me another tissue and then put her arms around me as we cried together. She moved both hands to my face to wipe away my tears, then kissed my cheeks.

"I can taste the salt in your tears," she mumbled, struggling to get the words out. "I taste your sadness, your regret. Put up a fight for me, dammit. Don't just slink away in shame."

I put my head down, afraid to look at her, but she lifted my chin with her forefinger. I tried to pull away, feeling unworthy of the intimacy, but she pulled me into her and kissed me.

"Kel…just let me leave, okay? I don't have the strength to resist you. Please."

She kissed me harder, darting her tongue into my mouth. Her hands were on both sides of my face, making sure I couldn't pull away. We were standing just a few feet away from the wall in her living room, and she forcefully guided us over to it. With my back against the wall, she pinned my arms up over my head, then pulled away from the kiss.

"Did you have an orgasm with her?"

I gasped at the question.

"Don't lie to me…please. Did you?" she repeated.

"I think so. It's all kind of a blur, but I think I did."

"Did she?"

"No. Maybe. I don't know. I remember touching her, but I don't think she came from that. She may have come on her own, though. I'm not sure. Why do you want to know this? Why create more pain by picturing the details of it all?"

"Because if I'm going to forgive you, I need to know what I'm forgiving. She went down on you?"

"Yes."

"And is that when you came?"

"Yes." Once again, the tears started flowing.

Kelly sighed. "Beth, look at me." I lifted my eyes to meet hers. Why did she have to have such beautiful eyes? "Do you want me? I don't mean just now, at this moment, while I'm kissing you. Do you want *all* of me, with everything that entails? The good, the bad—all of it. Do you want it?"

"I don't deserve it."

"That's not what I asked you. Do you want me?"

"When I woke up that morning and realized what I had done, all I could think of was losing my best friend, the woman I wanted to marry. The sense of self-loathing for sabotaging the best thing I've ever had was overwhelming."

"You are doing an excellent job of not answering my question. Why is that?"

"I guess it's because I no longer deserve the right to verbalize what I want."

"Oh, cut the self-deprecating bullshit, Beth." Kelly raised her voice in frustration. "It's a simple yes or no question."

"Yes, I want you. All of you."

"Good. Then show me. Fight for me. Do you want to marry me? Then be the person I think you are. The one who deserves to walk down that aisle with me. The one who made a mistake but admits it and learns from it."

"I did admit it. Jackie told me I was an idiot if I came over here and confessed, but I did because it was the right thing to do."

"Of course she did. Typical Jackie. Why be honest when a lie will do just as well?"

"I'm not Jackie," I said, somewhat indignantly and oblivious to the hypocrisy of the statement.

"I know you're not."

"Why are you even considering staying with me?"

"Because I love you, and I don't think one drunken night should destroy us."

"Kel..." I leaned into her and kissed her hard. I felt suddenly ravenous in the wanting of her. I turned us around so she was now the one with her back to the wall. She moaned in my ear while I kissed her neck. My hands reached under her T-shirt and caressed her breasts, but she abruptly pulled away.

"No. Not here, and not yet. I've been wallowing in Oreos and self-pity, and I need a shower. Give me ten minutes and meet me in the bedroom." She turned away and started to head toward the bathroom.

"Wait. Kelly?"

"What?"

"Do you want me too?" I asked sheepishly. "With all that that entails?"

She turned and walked back to stand in front of me, then put her arms around my waist, and said, "I want the dream you and I are supposed to have. The one I've been planning in my head since our second date. The one where we get to grow old together. Are you still the person from that dream?"

"Yes, I am."

"Good. Then you are the one I want. Wholly and completely."

* * * *

I waited for her nervously in her bedroom, listening to the water. I could see her silhouette through the frosted glass on the shower door. Her body was perfect. Perfect for me, that is. I never wanted a woman with a body like a model. I love women who look like real women—with beautiful curves and well-worn blemishes. Kelly's body showed her Irish heritage. She had freckles for days, and I could play connect the dots on any part of her body and still land on a spot that made me want to devour her. As she rinsed her shoulder-length blond hair in the shower, I took a breath, admiring her beauty and thinking about how lucky I was that she forgave me for my grievous error.

The sound of the water dwindled to a trickle, and she opened the shower door. As she leaned her head back to wring the water from her hair, she saw me from the corner of her eye. She grabbed her towel from the hook, never taking her eyes off me. I couldn't recall a time when I wanted her more than I did at that moment. Not even the first time, which was fraught with pent-up sexual frustration because she wouldn't sleep with me for the first three months after we started dating. She made me wait on purpose; she told me soon afterward. She wanted the desire to build. She didn't just want me to *want* her. I had to *need* her. And I did.

She used the towel to fluff her hair, then let it drop, her body still soaking wet. I felt like I couldn't catch my breath. She walked toward me with a hairbrush in her hand and sat down next to me. The water dripped off her hair, onto her shoulders, and down to her breasts.

"Will you brush my hair, please?" she asked. She turned her back to me. As I took the brush, I noticed my hand was shaking. She saw it too. "You're nervous?"

"I guess I am," I answered.

"Why is that? It's not like you've never seen me naked before."

I slowly ran the brush through her hair as I contemplated my response. "Maybe it's because I almost lost you. Maybe I never realized just how beautiful you are. And maybe I'm still thinking I don't deserve you."

She turned toward me, took the brush from my hand, and set it on the nightstand. She stood in front of me and guided me so my legs were still on the floor, but my back was flat on the bed.

"Why do you still have your clothes on?" she asked.

"I didn't want to be presumptuous."

"You mean the kiss I gave you downstairs didn't make it clear I want to fuck you?"

"If you keep talking to me like that, I will only last about thirty seconds before I come."

"Oh no. You don't get to do that. I want it long and slow." She undid my belt buckle and slowly unzipped my jeans. I lifted my hips and moved quickly to remove them, but she pushed me back down. "Long and slow, Bethany. Long and slow."

"Oh, now you're just taunting me by using my full name."

"Yes, I know." She reached inside the jeans and down into my underwear, and I whimpered at the touch. "I can feel the heat of you before I even touch you." She removed her hand, then grabbed mine to pull me into a sitting position. She pulled my T-shirt over my head and commanded me to take off my bra. Then she pushed me back onto the bed, staring at my breasts. Every nerve ending in my body responded to her gaze. She straddled me, her body still wet from the shower. I reached for her, but she wouldn't let me touch her.

"Not yet. Not until I say so," she whispered. She put her hands on my breasts and leaned down, her lips kissing my neck. She ran her tongue across my lips but stopped when I tried to kiss her. "Not yet. Not until I say so." She gently kissed each part of my face—my cheeks, my nose, my eyes. She ran her hands through my hair and playfully pulled on it, just enough to make sure I felt it. I needed to arch my back, but her weight on me made it impossible.

"Kelly…" I said breathlessly. "Please."

"Please what? Tell me, Beth. Tell me what you want. What do you want me to do—fuck you or make love to you?"

"Can't I have both?"

"No. Hard or soft? Strong or tender."

"Tender," I answered. As much as I wanted her to pound her fingers and her tongue into me, the need to feel her tender love for me was greater, given the vulnerabilities of the last few days.

She stood over me and finally released me from the constraints of my jeans. My legs were still on the floor with my back on the bed. I tried to move us both onto the bed, but she wouldn't allow it. She knelt on the floor before me, pushing her face between my legs. She teased me, gently blowing on me and softly kissing me, not allowing me to have what she knew I wanted.

I reached my hands toward the back of her head to push her into me, but that just made her lean back. "I will decide when to touch you," she said. She reached her hands behind my legs, cupping and caressing my ass. I lifted my hips in response, and she teased me with her tongue. I was soaking wet, and she moved her fingers to glide over me. She grabbed my hand and pressed it into me so I could feel it too. Then she took my fingers and put them in her mouth. I wanted to overpower her—take every part of her body into mine—but I knew how much she was enjoying this little game she was playing with me, so I suffered the torture of my as of yet unrequited lust.

"Bethany...look at me." I raised my head just enough to watch her. She leaned in and kissed my inner thigh, making her way up to take me into her mouth. My back arched in reflex as she finally ended the glorious misery. Her hands and tongue slowly worked together to ebb and flow my pleasure. Long and slow. When she felt that I was about to come, she slowed even more, letting it wash over me like the rolling tide—wave after gentle wave of gratification.

She moved her body up on top of me, kissing me along the way. I opened my eyes to look at her and saw tears in her eyes.

"Kel, what is it? What's wrong?" I pushed myself up onto my elbow and met her face to face. I put my hand on her cheek and wiped away the moisture.

"I love you," she cried.

"I love you, but you're sad all of a sudden. What is it?"

"I'm not sad. I'm in love. These are happy tears. I thought we were over. I thought you had left me, but here you are, and I'm seeing you and tasting you and smelling you, and I'm just...overwhelmed, that's all." She kissed me softly, then pushed me back down to rest her head in the crook of my arm. "Don't leave me again, okay?"

"Okay," I whispered.

"And don't sleep with any other women, okay?"

"Okay."

"I need to be enough for you."

"You are. More than enough."

"Actually, wait a minute. I take back what I just said about not leaving me. If I'm *not* enough for you, then be honest with yourself and leave. Don't stay unless I'm enough."

"You are all I want, Kelly. It was a stupid drunken mistake, and I'll regret it for the rest of my life. I don't want her—or any other woman, for that matter."

I pulled the covers up over her and caressed her hair as her breathing slowed. I wanted to take her and reciprocate the pleasure she had just given to me, but I could feel she was relaxing and sleep would not be far behind, so I let her be. She was spent from the emotions of the day, as was I. As painful as this time had been, it made me unquestionably certain that Kelly was the woman I was meant to marry.

Chapter Eleven

KELLY AND PAIGE CAME home from Christmas shopping to find Jackie curled up on the couch with a blanket. The television was on, but the sound was muted. Kelly tip-toed into the darkened living room and saw her eyes were closed, so she picked up the remote to turn it off.

"I was watching that." Jackie didn't open her eyes.

"Well, your eyes are closed, and there's no sound on, so I beg to differ, but okay. I'll leave it on." Kelly left the room searching for Beth, and Paige sat on the end of the couch by Jackie's feet.

"How are you feeling?"

"I'm fine. I was more tired than anything else." She took the blanket off and sat up. "I haven't been sleeping very well. Got a lot on my mind, I guess. How was after-Christmas shopping?"

"Good. We got some great bargains. Then we went out for a nice lunch—where you were supposed to meet us."

"I know. I'm sorry for bailing on you," Jackie said apologetically.

"It's okay, but your punishment for not showing up is that Kelly and I talked about you and Beth. She had a few stories to tell."

"Uh-oh. I'm sure she did not paint me in a very flattering light, no matter what story it was."

"Well, you're right. You did not exactly come out smelling like a rose."

"What did she tell you?" Jackie asked.

"She told me about the time you got Beth drunk and slept with her even though she was already with Kelly at the time."

"Oh." She lowered her head.

"I'm surprised my sister even lets you in this house, much less stay over. Assuming what she told me is true, that was a pretty shitty thing to do, Jackie."

"I'm sure what she told you was the truth. She doesn't have to exaggerate to make me seem shitty. The facts speak for themselves. I did it."

"Why?" Paige asked.

"I guess I was just jealous. We sat at dinner that night, and she could *not* stop talking about Kelly. Every conversation somehow came back to her. I think I just wanted to prove to her I still had a hold on her.

And I wasn't going to be able to do that if she was sober. So, I got her drunk and took advantage of her. The fact is that Beth and I had many problems when we were together, but sex was *not* one of them. I knew how to get to her."

"You almost destroyed them," Paige said judgmentally.

"I know. The shitty part of me wanted to break them up, but I'm not all bad, and I tried to make it right." Jackie stood up and went to the kitchen to get a beer. She came back with two and handed the other to Paige. They clinked bottles, and each took a swig. "Did Beth or Kelly tell you why I wanted to come here this week?"

"No. They're both pretty good at respecting other people's privacy. They probably figured it wasn't their place."

"True, although Kelly did tell you about this incident a few years ago, but anyway. The thing is I've been trying, many times unsuccessfully, to be a better person. I've realized it's time for me to grow up. Beth is the best grown-up I know, so I thought if I came here, it might help me, but even with good intentions, I did another stupid thing. I told Beth I wanted to come here because I was determined to get her back."

"And she *let* you come here?" Paige said, outraged.

"Yes, but before you judge her, let me finish. She told Kelly exactly what I had said and let Kelly make the final decision as to whether I could visit. I think Kelly, being the competitive person I know she is, took it as a challenge. Like, 'Okay, Jack. You think you can take her from me? Just try.' But the truth is I never really wanted to break them up. I just want what they have. They are who I want to be when I grow up."

"I get that."

"I thought maybe if I spent some time here—got away from my crazy life of sleeping with woman after woman—I might learn something."

"I hate to burst your bubble, but do you really think that good character is something that rubs off from one person to the next?"

"Well, to a certain extent, yes. Think about it. It's sort of like karma. Put good out into the world, and good comes back. If we see someone behaving a certain way and we admire that behavior, maybe we're inclined to model it."

"So, has Kelly figured out yet that you aren't trying to steal her wife?"

"Probably. I promised I would behave. Besides, we both know

she's too worried I'm going to sleep with you."

"Yeah. The whole purpose of telling me that story at lunch today was to show me you can't be trusted."

"I have to admit. It's good advice. I don't even trust myself. I can't expect anyone else to trust me."

"Are you afraid you'll pick up some random woman at the grocery store or something? And while you answer that question, can you tell me how you manage to get all these women to go to bed with you?"

She smiled and said, "Well, to answer the second question, I think I just have a way of telling a woman what she needs to hear in the moment. One moment leads to the next, and the next... As for the first question..." Jackie paused and took a deep breath. "I'm not afraid of a random woman. I'm afraid of you."

"Wait. What?"

"But don't worry. I made a promise, and I intend to keep it."
Paige blushed. "*Me?*"

"Yes, you. Is that so hard to imagine? I've only known you for two days, so it's probably a bit premature to speculate, but yeah...I could fall for you, Paige. Easily." She looked Paige in the eye sheepishly, waiting for her reaction. Before Paige could speak, Kelly and Beth came back into the room, breaking the trance. Jackie looked up and did a double take when she noticed Beth's hair was tousled.

"Nice hair, Beth. Geez. You two were apart for all of four hours. Did you miss each other that much?" Jackie laughed as she spoke.

"You're just jealous," Kelly said.

"Well, I think we've already established I'm jealous, but seeing you two jump each other in the middle of the afternoon makes it even worse."

Paige nervously got up from the couch and took the two empty beer bottles into the kitchen. She turned on the faucet and splashed water onto her hands, bringing them up to her face as discreetly as possible. She prayed for everyone to stay in the living room while she composed herself because the thought of starting something with Jackie was as scary as it was exhilarating.

Jackie came into the kitchen alone and opened the refrigerator absentmindedly. While she stood staring at the shelves stocked with food, she said, "You're looking a bit red in the face. I'm sorry, Paige. I shouldn't have said anything."

"We probably shouldn't discuss it with those two within hearing distance."

"Remember when I said I make bad decisions when it comes to women? Well, now you see what I mean." She closed the refrigerator door, went to her bedroom, and didn't appear again until dinner time.

Chapter Twelve

KELLY CAME HOME FROM shopping and found me in the bedroom folding laundry, my least favorite household chore in the world.

"Oh, good. You're home. That means I don't have to finish folding the rest of this basket, right? You know how bad I am at this."

"You have to fold the laundry *sometimes*, Beth. I think you do a crappy job on purpose, so I won't let you do it."

I continued folding, feeling sufficiently scolded. "How was shopping and lunch?" I asked.

"Good. We had a nice chat. I think I've convinced her to stay away from Jackie, so it was a successful afternoon."

That caught my attention, and I looked up from my basket of drudgery to see that she was smugly smiling. "How did you manage to do that?" I fumbled with a wrinkled T-shirt.

"Well, I didn't set out to tell her the story, but it came up in conversation. I told her how Jackie slept with you to try to break us up when we first got together. I was trying to point out she isn't to be trusted."

"I wish you had asked me before you did that. Now she'll think of me differently, knowing I cheated on you."

"No, I made it very clear you were coerced. I wasn't trying to make you look bad. I was trying to make Jackie look bad." She came over to me and moved the laundry basket out of the way. She could see I was displeased. I respected Paige's opinion and didn't want her to think less of me. That incident was the biggest regret of my life, and the fewer people who know about it, the better. Kelly put her arms around my neck and kissed me gently.

"I'm sorry, babe. You're right. I shouldn't have told that story without talking to you first. I just get the feeling those two have clicked, and it scares me. I hope the hard truth has sunk in, and she sees Jackie's true colors."

"No. It's okay. It's just that any mention of that time makes me angry with myself all over again, but it's your story too, and you have a right to tell it."

I put my arms around her and nuzzled into her neck for consolation. She smelled like her lavender soap, which I was convinced was laced with pheromones because I found it intoxicating. It never failed to turn me on, even at a moment like this when the conversation was heavy. I decided I would rather fool around with my wife than talk about the time I fooled around with someone else. So I reached for the top button of her shirt and made my way down, one by one.

"Beth," she said. I did not respond, preferring instead to persist in my attempt to get her on board with my sudden shift in desire.

"Earth to Beth." She tried again. "I see you are no longer participating in this conversation," she said, in a slightly breathy voice, which made it clear I was making some headway. "You have a very short attention span, you know that, babe?"

"Mmm…" I murmured.

"Okay, okay. I see I'm not going to have any further dialog with you until you've had your way with me." She fell back down on the bed. "I'm all yours."

"Mmm…" I murmured again, as I followed her onto the mattress and fondled her partially exposed breasts. The light from the window streamed down onto her face, and I paused to look at her.

"What?" she said, still in her breathy voice, wondering why I interrupted the foreplay.

"Nothing," I resumed the kissing.

It was her turn to pause now, and she gently pushed me just far enough away to look me in the eye. "Tell me. No talkie, no nookie."

I laughed out loud. "No nookie? What are you, twelve?"

Kelly laughed with me. "It was the first thing that came to mind."

"Okay. You'll think I'm corny, as usual, but the sunbeams highlight the touch of gold in your eyes and the mixture of light and dark blond in your hair, and I just needed to take a good long look. That's all. After all these years, I still can't figure out why you picked me. And why you didn't kick me to the curb when I fucked up."

"Do you want to talk about that time, or do you want to have sex with me?"

"The latter, please."

"I thought so. You can get lost in the sunbeams later. You got me all worked up, so could you give me what I want, please?" she said with some urgency.

"What do you want?" I climbed on top of her and balanced over her with arms outstretched on each side of her head. She reached for my face to pull me down into her, but I pulled up and out of her reach. "No talkie, no nookie. Tell me what you want." I lowered my face above her breasts, breathing heavily. I touched the tip of my tongue on her nipple, just enough to tease her.

She tugged at my shirt, pulling it over my head. "Take your bra off," she commanded. I obeyed and sat up with my legs straddling her at the waist. She reached up, caressed my breasts, and pulled herself up to take them into her mouth. "I want those pants off. Now." I could tell she wanted to be in control, so I quickly hopped off her and did as she asked. I unbuckled her belt and repeated the process with her.

She stood to meet me, pressing our naked bodies together, then turned me around and bent me over so my upper body was face down on the bed. She reached for me from behind, pushing the fingers of her right hand into me while her left hand groped to reach for my breast. I pressed my face into the duvet, moaning as she fucked me with her fingers. She continued until she felt me getting near my orgasm, then stopped.

She sat on the floor between my legs, her back against the bed. I started to move, thinking she wanted me on the floor with her, but she held me there, my legs still standing and facing her, my upper body still bent at the waist on the bed. She pushed my legs apart, reached her hands to spread me wide open, and dove her tongue into me. I crushed my face further into the bed covers to keep our visitors from hearing my cries of ecstasy. When my legs could no longer hold me up, she guided me down into her lap, taking me into her arms to hold me while the aftershocks continued to electrify me.

As I caught my breath, she looked into my eyes and said, "That..." she kissed me softly before continuing, "is one of the many reasons I didn't kick you to the curb, my love."

Chapter Thirteen

THAT EVENING, JACKIE GOT a call from an old friend who invited her for a drink. Left to our own devices, the three of us sat at the table playing cards. I was winning and had decided to call it a night, three dollars richer than I was two hours earlier. Besides, my wife had worn me out that afternoon. My legs felt like jelly, and I was exhausted. I was about to get up to leave the room when Paige dropped a bombshell on us.

"I think I want to ask Jackie out to dinner," she said nonchalantly. Kelly had just taken a sip of her tea, and she choked on it, spitting it all over the table.

"You must be joking," she said with as much disgust as she could muster. We each grabbed a napkin to soak up the liquid.

"I'm not joking. I like her. I think we'd have fun together."

"Okay, first of all, she's probably fucking some random girl in the bathroom of a bar as we speak. Secondly, didn't we *just* spend the afternoon discussing the shitty things she has done over the years? Thirdly, you've known her for all of ten minutes. Are you fucking kidding me?" Kelly was red in the face and close to shouting at this point. I reached for her hand to calm her down, which seemed to make things worse, and she jerked it away from me.

"Kel, I know you're trying to protect me, and I appreciate it, but I've been sufficiently warned—by you and her. Maybe I just want to have a little fun. I'm not saying I'm going to marry her. I want to take her out on a date. I haven't had a date in a year and a half. You keep bugging me to move on with my life, so here I am...moving on."

"No, no, no...that is not how I wanted you to move on! Please, Paige. Reconsider this. Did she talk you into this?"

"No, she hasn't done anything out of line. She's been an angel, just like she promised you she would be. She has no idea I'm even considering this. I wanted to tell you about it without her here so you wouldn't blame her when it happened. Kelly, I'm thirty-four years old. I'm perfectly capable of making my own decisions. You've done your job—you warned me. I get it. She's not perfect."

I had been sitting quietly, letting them hash it out, but given I had a lot of experience in this matter, I debated weighing in on it. If I encouraged it, my wife would surely make me pay for it later. On the other hand, I had seen some signs of growth in Jackie, and maybe Paige would be good for her.

"Can I comment on this, ladies?" I asked tentatively. I knew Paige wouldn't mind, but I expected Kelly to shoot me a look of pure evil. To my surprise, she did just the opposite.

"Babe, please do. Maybe you can talk some sense into her. Tell Paige about what you had to put up with when you were with Jackie, how she cheated on you multiple times, how she lied, and how she broke your heart. Tell her."

I took a deep breath, knowing that what I was about to say would probably not go over very well.

"Yes, Paige. All of those things and more are true. Jackie has made her share of mistakes, and I paid the price for many of them, but..."

Kelly slapped her hand down on the table. "That's it. Full stop. There is no 'but...'"

"Kel, let me finish, okay? There is a *but*. That was eleven years ago. We've all grown up a lot since then. She's taken a little longer than most to come around, but I think she's trying."

"Oh, please. That's bullshit. She came here this week to convince you to get back together with her."

"She didn't really mean that," I said.

"Of course she did!"

Paige chimed in. "No, she told me about that. She said her real intent in coming here was to spend time around people she respects and wants to be like. She said it's time for her to grow up, and since Beth is the best grown-up she knows, coming here for a while might help her."

"She said that?" Kelly asked.

"Yes. She said you guys are who she wants to be when she grows up."

"I don't buy it," Kelly barked, as she got up from the table.

"It's not for you to 'buy,' Kel. If I want to take her to dinner to get to know her, that's my prerogative."

As Paige spoke, we could hear the key in the front door lock, and Jackie made her way into the dining room. "Hey, y'all." She scanned the room to look at each of us, and the smile left her face. "Whoa. There is some seriously bad energy in this room right now. What's happening here?"

Kelly stood up and started to clear the table. "Ask Paige," she said, as she stormed out of the room. Jackie gave Paige a WTF look, trying to figure out precisely what she had stumbled upon.

"My sister is upset with me because I told her I wanted to ask you out on a date with me."

"Wait. What?" Jackie asked, trying very hard to hide a smile. Knowing her as well as I did, I could see this revelation was pleasantly intriguing for her. She paused, choosing her words carefully to avoid Kelly's wrath. "Paige, as much as I would love to go out with you, I will respectfully decline."

Paige's expression wilted like a week-old rose. "Oh...okay," she said meekly. Kelly came back into the room and stared at Jackie. "Are you happy, Kel? She turned me down."

"Listen..." Jackie said. "I made a promise to Beth and Kelly. You're off-limits. They don't trust me with you, and I don't blame them. I think you're awesome, and under any other circumstances, I would go out with you in a heartbeat, but I'm not going to break my promise."

Kelly looked on incredulously. I smiled at her, trying to convey my 'See? I told you she was growing up,' sentiment, and I think the message was received because her anger immediately dissipated, and she lowered her eyes to avoid the look she was getting from Paige.

"Jackie," Paige said. "Would you like to go to dinner with me?"

Jackie looked around the room, unsure of what to say. Paige continued. "You know I love my sister and would do almost anything to make her happy, but I'm a grown-ass woman who can decide who I go out with. So I will ask you again. Jackie, would you like to go to dinner with me?"

Jackie looked at Kelly for direction, and Paige grabbed her hand. "Kelly is not asking you out, Jackie. I am. She doesn't get to dictate your answer."

Kelly shrugged her shoulders as if to say, 'I give up.'

"I think I would really like that, Paige," Jackie said in a voice that was equal parts scared and excited.

"Great. Tomorrow night. Dress nice. I'm going to bed. Goodnight, all." As she left the room, she went over to Kelly, hugged her, and whispered something in her ear.

Jackie looked back and forth between us, not knowing what she was supposed to say at this point. She knew Kelly was upset and didn't want to make it worse. "Kelly, I swear I didn't..." She put her hands up in surrender.

"I know. I know. I'm not mad at you. But here's the thing, Jackie. If you hurt my sister, you will have to deal with me. Understood?"

"Understood." She turned to leave the room. "Goodnight, you two."

Chapter Fourteen

JACKIE STOOD AT THE bathroom mirror, checking for wrinkles and lint on her shirt and pants. When she was satisfied everything checked out, she did one last touch-up to her hair, then reached for the jacket on the back of the chair. She straightened the collar, making sure everything was perfect. On her final glance in the mirror, she noticed perspiration on her upper lip, which she quickly blotted with a tissue. She paused momentarily, remembering the last time she was nervous about going on a date. Never. This was a new experience for her—one she didn't know what to make of and wasn't quite sure she enjoyed. Confidence gave Jackie an edge whenever she was with a woman, and she was afraid nerves would be a confidence killer for her.

As she reached for her phone and keys from the nightstand, she heard the doorbell, followed by the security system of Jake and Olly barking. Jackie yelled across the hall for Paige to answer the door since Kelly and Beth had gone out to a movie. With no answer from Paige and the doorbell ringing again, she went to the door to see who was interrupting her date preparations. She opened the door quickly so it would be apparent to the visitor she was in a hurry and wanted no part of whatever they were selling. But to her surprise, she found Paige standing on the threshold, holding a beautiful bouquet of fresh roses.

"Paige, why are you ringing the doorbell? You have a key."

"I'm here to pick up my date, and I wanted to do it properly. These are for you." Paige handed the roses to Jackie. "Are you ready to go, or may I come in?"

Jackie was caught off guard, not expecting the romantic gesture of calling for her at the door, as if she was old-school courting her. Never one to blush, Jackie was even more surprised to feel a rush of heat to her cheeks. "Um…yeah, okay. Come in. I just need another minute. Let me put these in some water."

Paige trailed behind her as she went to the kitchen to rummage around for a vase. Once the flowers were appropriately situated in their new watery home, Jackie again reached for her phone and keys, and they made their way to Paige's rental car. Paige followed Jackie to the passenger side, opened the door, and helped her into the seat.

"Wow, I'm really getting the special 'date' treatment, huh? I kinda like this. I'm usually the one in the proverbial driver's seat. This is nice for a switch."

Paige returned to her side of the car and settled behind the wheel. "Well, get used to it. Since I'm the one who asked you out, I get to be the one in charge."

"So, where are we going?"

"I made us a reservation at a steakhouse called Larsen's. You're not a vegetarian, are you?"

"No, I'm not. Larsen's gets wonderful reviews, so that should be really nice. I'm impressed."

"It bodes well for me if just making a reservation impresses you." Paige turned to Jackie and smiled, then backed the car out of the driveway.

"Paige, I saw your rental car yesterday. It was a Ford Focus. This is a Lexus. Did you steal a car this afternoon while I was busy getting ready for our date?"

"Picking you up in a Ford Focus would not have been in line with the ambiance I was hoping to portray this evening. I went over to Avis this morning to swap it out."

"I'm impressed again. Or still, I should say."

"Good. Sit back, though, because there's more to come." Paige turned on the satellite radio and chose the coffee house station, remembering Jackie said she liked the singer-songwriter style. They made small talk on the way to the restaurant, then arrived at the door with a valet ready to open their doors and take the keys.

Paige led them through the crowd to the hostess stand and said, "Hi. We have a reservation for two at seven. It's under Gallagher and Fairburn."

"Yes, ma'am, follow me, please," the hostess replied.

"Nice touch, Paige. I didn't even know you knew my last name," Jackie said, as they followed her to their table.

"I'm not one to take a woman out on a date if I don't know her last name. Besides, I needed to know what it was so I could Google you and find out everything there is to know about you."

"Ah, I see. And did you find what you needed to know?"

"Yes, you're not a criminal. That's all I needed to know." They were seated in a semi-private room with only three other tables, spread far apart in the expansive area. The waiter came over to meet them as they sat and asked if they needed anything to drink.

"Yes, please. Can we have a bottle of champagne?" Paige asked. He nodded and left to retrieve it. "I hope you like champagne," she said. "Maybe I should have checked before I ordered it."

"Not to worry. I love champagne. So far, you're batting a thousand."

The waiter returned and popped the cork, poured their glasses, and returned the bottle to its ice bucket. He asked, "Would you ladies like to hear the specials?"

"I think we'd like to sit for a while before we do that. We're in no rush," Paige said. He left the table, and she raised her glass for a toast. "Here's to...hmmm. What should we drink to, Jackie?"

"How about new experiences?"

"Perfect. Here's to new experiences. May we both enjoy them." The glasses clinked, and they each took a sip.

Paige reached for the menu, but Jackie put her hand on hers and gently pushed the menu back onto the table. "There's time for that. First, I have a few questions."

"Okay. Go for it."

"What is all this, Paige? What's happening here?"

"It's a date. Perhaps you are familiar with the concept?" she replied sarcastically.

"I am, indeed, but I get the feeling this is out of character for you. Why are you trying so hard to impress me? You didn't need to rent a luxury car. We didn't have to come to a fancy place and have champagne."

"I'm trying to turn the tables on you. I know you're usually the player, so I'm making sure we establish right off the bat that you are *not* the player here. And neither am I. I'm just a woman who finds you interesting and attractive, and I wanted to take you out for a nice evening to get to know you. How do you feel about that?"

"I'm intrigued. And flattered. Make sure you tell your sister I was not the one doing the 'playing' tonight, okay?" She made air quotes as she spoke.

"My sister is not here tonight. This is just you and me."

Jackie took a deep breath. "Yes. You and me. So, are you usually this forthright when you go out on dates?"

"I don't date much. I haven't been on a date in forever. So I guess the answer is no. You must have some effect on me."

"Why don't you date much, Paige? I mean, you're smart and funny, and you're drop-dead gorgeous. I can't imagine you have much trouble meeting people."

"Meeting people isn't a problem. Meeting people I think are worth the effort is more of a problem. I'm selective. And any details beyond that are a story for another day."

"In that case, I'm honored I've passed your selection process."

"I'm flattered you think I'm gorgeous."

"I said drop-dead gorgeous. That's a level above gorgeous."

"Now you're just making me blush." Paige looked down shyly.

"I know. The redness on your cheeks makes your eyes even bluer. And when you pushed your hair behind your ear just now, I could see the tip of your ear is red too, which is so adorable I can't stand it."

"Adorable? That's not exactly what I was going for. Adorable is great for a seven-year-old girl, not a thirty-four-year-old woman."

"Ah. Never underestimate the power of adorable, Paige. I'll take that characteristic any day of the week. You keep that up, and you will bring me to my knees. I don't stand a chance."

"Yeah, right. The inimitable Jackie Fairburn isn't likely to be brought to her knees by any woman."

"You aren't just any woman," Jackie replied.

"You're flattering me again, Jackie."

"No, I'm being honest. Flattery implies I'm saying something nice about you to get something I want from you. I'm just speaking the truth. There is something about you, Paige. I know you know all about my reputation." Jackie lowered her head in an embarrassed gesture. "And maybe I could prove that reputation to be true by turning on the charm and convincing you to sleep with me, but that is not what I want from you, Paige. I hope that's not what you want from me. I want to get to know you, to figure you out."

"It's not what I want from you," Paige responded. "Well, to be clear, it's not *all* I want from you." She reached across the table for Jackie's hand.

Jackie squirmed in her seat at the implication of Paige's clarifying statement. "You know, as I was getting ready this afternoon, I promised myself I would be a good girl and I wouldn't do anything physical with you tonight. You're making that harder and harder as we go."

"Good. That means the evening is going according to plan."

* * * *

After the dinner plates had been cleared and the coffee was served, the waiter gave them each a fork to share the piece of flourless chocolate cake he set down on the table between them. Paige dove right in while Jackie hesitated.

"Why aren't you indulging in this with me?" Paige asked.

"I'm enjoying watching you eat it."

"Oh, right. I'm sure it's very attractive to see me shove a hunk of cake into my mouth."

"You have no idea how attractive it is."

Paige took a sip of her coffee, then pierced the cake with her fork. She lifted it as if she was going to eat it and then redirected it to Jackie. "Let me see for myself," Paige said, prompting Jackie to open her mouth. She shook her head when she removed the now cake-less fork from Jackie's mouth. "Hmmm...You've got a point there. Very sexy." She lowered her fork and stared at Jackie while she finished swallowing the sweet treat.

"What?" Jackie asked.

"I want to kiss you."

"Here? Now? While I have chocolate frosting all over my mouth?" She picked up her napkin to wipe her lips, only to have Paige reach for her hand to stop her.

"Yes. Here and now." She leaned over to Jackie and tenderly kissed her, tasting the chocolate on her lips. "I've been wanting to do that all night."

"Paige..."

Paige kissed her again, and Jackie pulled away this time. "Is something wrong?" Paige asked.

"No. Your kiss is even better than I imagined it would be, but I'm not very good at just kissing, and if we go much further, I'm going to break that promise to myself that we discussed earlier."

"Did you make that promise just to prove to my sister you wouldn't sleep with me?"

"No. I made that promise to myself because I don't want you to be just another woman I sleep with. I want it to mean something with you."

"Okay, so how long do I have to wait to sleep with you to have it mean something?"

"You aren't making this easy, are you, Paige?"

"Just trying to understand the rules."

"There are no rules. I just wanted it to be different with you. I care about you, Paige."

"Okay, then make it different."

"What do you mean?"

"*Be* different. Don't sleep with me, and get up and leave right afterward. Don't treat me the way you might treat some other women you've been with. For as long as you are with me, be with *just* me. Show me you care about me."

"Okay. I can do that."

"Good. Can you do that and still let me make love to you tonight? Because I *need* to be with you tonight. I need you to stay with me and wake up with me in the morning. Does that frighten you, Jackie?"

"It terrifies me." She lowered her head in response.

"Look at me, Jackie. Is it too much to ask of you?"

"No, it's not."

"Good. I want to take you to a hotel, okay? I don't want to be worried about making too much noise or my sister's prying eyes. I'll send her a text so she doesn't worry about us."

Jackie smiled and sat back in her chair as Paige paid the check and made a hotel reservation on her phone. Her heart was pounding against her chest, thinking about the night to come. Paige had surprised her at every turn, and the night was only half over. She just prayed she had the wherewithal to be the person Paige thought she could be.

Chapter Fifteen

WHEN THEY ARRIVED AT the Marriott hotel in downtown Atlanta, Jackie smiled as Paige explained to the woman at the check-in counter that they had not even one single piece of luggage. The woman gave them a knowing look to go along with their card key and pointed them to the elevators. As they ascended, Paige pinned Jackie against the oak-paneled elevator wall and kissed her passionately, giving Jackie a preview of what was to come. The car stopped, and the doors opened on the fifth floor. A couple was about to enter but thought better of it when they saw Paige and Jackie kissing. "Sorry," they both said, and let the doors close behind them.

As they exited on floor eleven and made their way to their room, Paige tugged at Jackie's hand and rushed her to the room, anxious to get her alone. She closed the door behind them, and they each nervously removed their coats and shoes.

"I'm nervous," Paige said, nearly out of breath.

"Really? You could have fooled me. You've been nothing but confident all evening."

"That's mostly an act. Inside, I'm scared to death."

"What are you afraid of?" Jackie asked.

"You. How I feel about you. How much I want you."

"Does it help to know I'm afraid of the same things?"

"A little, but you're much more experienced at this than I am. I feel like I don't know what I'm doing."

"You've done every single thing right so far tonight." Jackie came closer to Paige and put her arms around her neck. She leaned in for a tender kiss, trying to slow things down from the frenzy of the elevator. "You seemed to enjoy being the one in control tonight. If you're scared, would you rather I take over for a little while?" Paige nodded, and a weight seemed to lift. "Okay. Just relax. We're both nervous. There's no rush. I want to be here with you. Do you want me to order us something to drink?"

"No. I want my head clear. I want to remember this."

"Do you mind if we slow it down a little bit? I don't want this to feel like a hotel booty call. Don't get me wrong, Paige. I want you, probably more than I can adequately say using just words. It's just that I'd like to savor it a bit."

"I don't mind at all. Sorry I attacked you in the elevator. Guess I got a little over-excited."

"I'm right there with you, believe me. You are standing right in front of me—willing—and my instinct is to dive right into you."

"Jackie, I haven't felt this way in a very long time. Years, if I'm being honest. I'm scared, and I'm excited, and I'm having a little trouble catching my breath."

Jackie took Paige's hand and led her over to the gray and white patterned sofa. She went to the mini-bar and took two bottles of water, pouring each into a glass. She handed one to Paige, sat next to her, and took a drink of her own. Then she pulled Paige into her, with her head in the crook of Jackie's arm. She caressed Paige's hair and whispered, willing them both to relax.

"You don't need to be scared of me, Paige. I'm not going to hurt you. There are a million things I don't know about you, and I want to spend time checking things off of that list."

"What is one thing you want to know about me right now?"

"Just one thing, huh? Okay. This is an important one, so answer carefully. Do you or do you not like *Friends*?"

Paige lifted her head and looked at Jackie in confusion. "As in the television show?"

"Yes."

"I can quote almost every *Friends* episode by heart."

"Oh, I *knew* you were the woman for me!" Jackie leaned in and kissed her.

"That's all it takes to be the woman for you, huh? Who knew it was that easy."

"Well, it's not only that, but it helps. A lot."

"What else do you want in your one ideal woman, Jackie?"

"It's funny. I've never really given it much thought because I never thought I wanted one woman, but that's been changing lately, so I guess...let's see...she needs to be sexy. Confident, for sure. Smart. Intelligence is a major turn-on, but mostly, she needs to be kind, not just to me but to those around her. Kindness to animals and the planet is also a requirement."

"Right, I can see you haven't given this *any* thought!"

"I guess maybe I've known it all along and just needed someone to ask me." Jackie turned Paige's face to look at her. "You are all of those things, Paige."

She leaned in and kissed her sweetly. She could hear Paige's soft, throaty murmur, and she pulled her in closer and increased the intensity of her kiss. Paige reached up, put her hand on Jackie's cheek, and twisted her body so she was facing her. Jackie darted her tongue in and out of Paige's mouth, running it across her lips.

Paige straddled her with her knees on the couch on either side of Jackie's waist as they kissed feverishly. Jackie reached behind her, held her tightly under her ass, and picked her up while Paige wrapped her legs around Jackie's back. She carried her over to the bed and put her down on it, laying down on top of her. Paige reached up to touch Jackie's breast through her shirt while Jackie kissed her neck.

"Paige..." she whispered in her ear. She pulled her face away from Paige's and asked, "Are you sure this is what you want?"

"I don't think I've ever wanted anyone more."

Jackie stood up and pulled Paige to a sitting position. She unbuttoned the first few buttons of her blouse, then pulled it over Paige's head, exposing her beautiful breasts cupped in a lacy lavender bra. Jackie undid the clasp of her pants, stepped out of them, then pulled her shirt over her head, taking her bra with it in the same effortless motion.

Jackie gently leaned Paige backward, lowered the zipper on her pants, and pulled them off slowly. She reached behind Paige and undid the clasp of her bra. Jackie guided them back onto the bed, and Paige rolled over on top of her, kissing her passionately. "Paige..." Jackie whispered. "I want you."

"You have me. Take whatever you want."

Jackie kissed Paige's breast and put it in her mouth, sucking while Page arched her back for more. Jackie kissed her neck and her arms, and her torso. She rolled Paige over onto her stomach and kissed her back and her ass, feeling her way as she moved. While Paige was still face down, Jackie laid on top of her, breasts to back. She kissed the back of her neck and whispered in her ear, telling her how beautiful and sexy she was. Paige moaned with pleasure, begging to be touched.

"Get up on your knees," Jackie commanded. Paige did as she was told, facing away from Jackie in a doggie-style position. Jackie reached from behind and slipped easily across her slit, finding the spot that made Paige squirm. She focused there just long enough to build the excitement, then flipped Paige onto her back. Jackie dove her tongue into Paige, feeling the waves building. She took her fingers and entered her, keeping her tongue in place in constant motion. Paige screamed in ecstasy and came on command when Jackie told her she wanted it.

As she started to calm from the first orgasm, Jackie returned for another, taking her ravenously until Paige had to pull away because the intensity was too much. They breathed heavily into each other, Jackie taking her into her arms and holding her as tight as she could while Paige caught her breath and finally stopped quivering.

Jackie waited a moment, then got up to go into the bathroom. She ran the warm water, soaked a washcloth, then wrung it out. She returned to the bed with the cloth in hand and placed it between Paige's legs, resting the wet warmth on her and gently rubbing her with the cloth, cleaning and stroking her. Paige opened her legs wider and moaned softly, enjoying the sensation of the heat and the moisture. When the cloth had cooled down, Jackie took it away and threw it to the floor. She climbed back under the covers and pulled Paige into her arms.

"Hey," Jackie said after a few minutes.

"Hey," Paige repeated, still catching her breath.

"Are you okay?" Jackie asked.

"I think I'm in shock."

"Is that a good thing?"

"What do you think?"

"Well, I can only go by the looks of things from my vantage point, but I think it's a good thing, yes."

"Nice touch with the hot cloth. That might be the sexiest thing anyone has ever done after sex. I'll bet all your women love that."

Jackie made a sound indicating the mention of other women at that moment was a bit of a jab she was unprepared for.

"I'm sorry, Jack. I shouldn't have said that."

"It's alright. I understand. But for the record, I've never done that with anyone before."

"What made you do it with me?" Paige asked, sitting up and resting on her elbow.

"I'm not sure. I guess I wanted to keep touching you, and it seemed like something you might enjoy."

"Well, it worked. I think I was still throbbing."

"You were. It was beautiful. I'm in awe of your body. I could get lost in you."

Paige looked up into Jackie's eyes. She felt so many new things, but sensed it was much too soon to verbalize them. Jackie seemed to understand the look and guided her back down to lay in the crook of her arm. She rubbed her arm absent-mindedly while Paige gently caressed her breasts.

"Go to sleep, Paige. You look so tired."

"Not tired, per se. Just pleasantly spent. And oddly still a bit wired. It's a strange combination."

"Let the spent feeling take over and drift off to sleep. I'm not going anywhere."

"But what about you? Don't I get a chance to get lost in your body too?"

"There's plenty of time for that. Besides, do you think you could have an orgasm like that, and I wouldn't have come along with you?"

"I don't know your body well enough yet. Some people don't come that easily."

"I'm normally one of those people. I am more of a giver than a taker."

"But you came with me?"

"Yes. There was no way I could watch you and not have an orgasm. You are quite breathtaking."

"Sex faces are hardly breathtaking. Now you're just trying to flatter me."

Jackie sat up, turned to face Paige, and put her hand under her chin to raise her to eye level. "No. I'm not," she said with determination. "I know you think I use a line like that with all the women, just like you said, but I don't. If I'm being truthful, I don't usually say much at all." She paused. "But Paige? You are *breathtaking*. Do you believe me?"

Paige drew in her breath, looked Jackie in the eyes, and nodded yes.

"Good." She pulled Paige down into her and held her close until Paige fell asleep. As Jackie listened to the measured breathing beside her, her heart started racing. This was a new experience, and she wasn't sure what to make of it.

Chapter Sixteen

IN A GESTURE THAT shocked no one, Kelly paced on the outside patio the following day, pretending to tend to the few plants that remained from the previous season. She occasionally threw the ball to the dogs, giving her an excuse to walk around the lawn when they didn't retrieve it.

I sat wrapped in a sweatshirt and blanket in my lounge chair, measuring her frustration and trying to determine what it would take to keep her from killing Jackie. She'd read the text from Paige while we were lying in bed watching the baseball game the previous night. She simply put her phone down, turned off her light, and said, "Paige and Jackie are not coming home tonight. They're staying in a hotel." Then she rolled over in the darkness and didn't say another word.

While Kelly continued her charade, I heard a bling on my phone and saw it was a text from Paige. I also noticed it was only sent to me, not on the group text thread we started a few days ago. I discreetly read her message while I flipped the switch to put the phone on vibrate only.

> Paige: Almost home. So, what are we walking into?
> Beth: A hornet's nest.
> Paige: Do I need to get a bulletproof vest for Jackie?
> Beth: Probably not a bad idea.
> Paige: How am I going to convince her that Jackie didn't do this? I did.
> Beth: Just tell her the truth. And tell Jackie to keep her mouth shut. BTW, what is the truth, exactly?
> Paige: I'm falling for her.
> Beth: OMG. Do not say those words to Kelly. Did you say them to Jackie?
> Paige: Not yet.
> Beth: Good. Jackie is a known flight risk. And it's too soon!
> Paige: I know how I feel, Beth.
> Beth: What you feel right now is endorphin-induced. Sex will do that to you.
> Paige: Great sex.
> Beth: I didn't need to know that. Paige, please. Slow down.
> Paige: I'll try. No promises. See you in a few.

* * * *

       I put the phone back in my pocket and mentally prepared myself for the coming onslaught of *What Were You Thinking*s and *How Could You*s. I was praying Paige could come up with something better than, "I'm falling for her."

       Our yard was situated such that it was possible to see the driveway from the back left corner, which is where Kelly happened to be when she saw a Lexus pull into our driveway. She headed out the side gate and made her way out front, so I followed her to see what was happening. Paige and Jackie were exiting the car when we rounded the corner, and I could already see confusion from Kelly when she saw the Ford Focus was nowhere to be found. Instead, the bright December sun accentuated the cobalt blue Lexus.

       "Nice car, Paige. Did you steal it or something?"

       "Yes. Grand theft is my new hobby. That, and staying in swanky hotels with Jackie, of course."

       I had to hand it to Paige. As usual, she knew exactly how to disarm her sister. Kelly smiled as she often did when Paige gave her a smart-ass response. I was starting to wish I had popcorn to watch this conversation unfold.

       "Are we going to talk about this like adults?" Kelly asked.

       "What's to talk about? As an adult, I exercised my prerogative to take Jackie out for a nice dinner and spend the night with her at a hotel. As you can see, we've both lived to tell the tale. There's not much else to discuss, as I don't plan to give you the details."

       Jackie stood by looking uncomfortable, which was unusual for her, given that she's a pretty take-charge kind of girl. Maybe Paige told her I said she should keep her mouth shut.

       "Where did the car come from?"

       "I went over to Avis yesterday and swapped it out. I wanted something nicer for our date." Paige grinned a big toothy grin as she said this and looked over at Jackie.

       "I have to admit. It was a very nice touch," Jackie said.

       "Jackie, can you stay out of this, please?"

       "I think I'm pretty much 'in' it, Kelly. I was there with her—all night."

       "Yeah, but you won't be for too long."

       "I know you think that's true, but as they say, past results are not always indicative of future performance. One thing is true, though. I care about your sister very much. And that, in and of itself, is a differentiator for me in this situation. I didn't orchestrate any of what happened last night."

Kelly sighed in acceptance of this new reality. "So what happens now?"

Paige chimed in. "Nothing specific. We'll just live in the moment and enjoy the ride. Tonight is New Year's Eve. I think we should go to the market, pick up enough food and drink for a feast, then come back home and toast to our good fortune in the new year.

"Listen, Kel, I didn't do this to piss you off. This wasn't about you. It's about me, doing something for myself that I felt like I wanted and needed to do. I don't want you to be upset with me. I need you in my corner, always. I'm not sure where I'd be in my life without you, and I don't want to find out. Please don't let this come between us. I'm happy right now. Will I be happy forever? Who knows? Nobody can predict that, not even you. But I'm stronger than you give me credit for, and even if Jackie takes off tomorrow, I will be fine."

Jackie took some offense to that remark and started to respond when Paige cut her off. "Jackie, let's face it. It could happen. I don't want it to happen, but it could. Kel, the point is I'm not the fragile eighteen-year-old who watched her girlfriend get killed. That girl is long gone. She grew up a long time ago."

Kelly walked over to Paige, put her hands on her cheeks, and lowered her head so she could kiss her forehead. "I will always be in your corner. I promise. And Jackie, I will repeat what I said yesterday. You will have to deal with me if you hurt my baby sister. That said, I will tell you this. If Paige has decided she wants to be with you, then you should consider yourself a very lucky girl."

"I came to that realization about halfway through the appetizer course last night," Jackie responded and reached for Paige's hand as they walked into the house.

Chapter Seventeen

WHEN THE FOUR OF them returned to the house, Jackie and Paige went to their respective rooms to change their clothes from the prior evening. After a few minutes, Jackie knocked on Paige's door, hoping to sneak in a few minutes of alone time before regrouping with Kelly and Beth for their New Year's Eve shopping excursion.

"Knock, knock. Are you decent?"

"Do you want me to be decent?" Paige answered, opening the door.

"Well, I'd certainly be quite pleased to see you indecent, but I'll take you any way I can."

"Had you come in two minutes ago, you would have gotten your way." Paige reached for Jackie's hand and drew her in closer. The morning after in the hotel had been exhilarating. They made love, ordered room service breakfast, made love again, and then took a shower together before it came time to check out. Paige was playing it cool on the outside, but in her heart, she loved every minute of her time with Jackie, which made her a little nervous.

Jackie put her arms around her, kissed her softly, and nuzzled her neck. "I love the way you handle your sister. You seem to know exactly how to approach her."

"It comes from thirty-four years of practice. She means well, and I know she only wants the best for me."

Jackie lifted her head to look Paige in the eye. "You said something earlier that caught me off guard."

"I did? What's that?"

"You said you saw your girlfriend get killed."

"Ah...I guess I did say that." Paige tensed, pulled herself out of their embrace, and turned away.

"Do you want me to pretend I didn't hear that?" Jackie asked, hoping the answer would not be a yes.

Paige started a slow pace around the room. "It's not something I talk about. There are probably only about four people in my life who know about it."

"Okay. I understand if I don't fall into that category. I just wanted to let you know I heard it, and I'm here if you want to talk about it." Jackie moved toward the door, clearly hurt by Paige's insinuation that she was not yet part of her inner circle of confidants.

Paige met her at the door. "Wait. I didn't say I wouldn't tell you."

"No, but you implied it was private."

"You didn't give me a chance. It's just not an easy story to tell. And I'm not sure I'm in the right mindset to tell it today. Is that okay?"

"Of course it is. I am in no position to dictate what you do and do not talk to me about, Paige, but I hope we can get to the point where you feel comfortable sharing with me. I really want to get to know you."

"I feel the same. Let's just take it a little at a time, okay? It's New Year's Eve. I want to end the year on a good note and start the new one with hope, not sorrow. If you and I enjoy each other's company and decide to explore whatever this thing is with us, then there will be time enough for life stories on another day. Is that fair?"

"That's more than fair," Jackie agreed.

"Good. Now, I believe you were kissing my neck. Where did we leave off with that?"

"We have about a minute and a half before your sister and her wife start looking for us. I don't think we can accomplish much in that amount of time."

"You'd be surprised. At the very least, I'm sure you could find a way to make me look forward to coming back here later and ringing in the year with you."

Jackie pulled Paige into her arms and kissed her softly, guiding her tongue across Paige's lips. Paige put her hands on the back of Jackie's head, pulling her in closer. She started guiding them toward the bed when they heard Kelly calling them from down the hall.

"Mmm..." Paige murmured. "Don't forget where we were. We will continue this later."

Chapter Eighteen

THE FOUR OF US went to Whole Foods and spent a ridiculous amount of money on our New Year feast. I decided I wanted chicken wings, but Kelly and Jackie opted for breads, cheeses, and more snacks than we could consume in a week. As we went through the checkout line, I reflected on our good fortune, having the means to indulge in this much food while ringing in the new year with people I love.

I watched Kelly as she made small talk with the cashier. Her kindness never ceased to amaze me, and I marveled at her ability to talk to anyone who crossed her path. I didn't possess that skill, instead preferring to keep to myself in most situations, but I envied her because she opened herself up to so many more experiences than I did by simply starting a conversation with a stranger. We learned the cashier—her name was Joan—was a single mother of two, and she was anxious to get home to ring in the new year with her kids, who had just returned from visiting their father for Christmas.

Kelly recommended some television station she heard was doing their version of "Dick Clark's New Years' Rockin' Eve" for kids. I didn't even know such a thing existed and didn't give it much thought until Paige and Jackie decided they wanted to watch that show rather than be subjected to Ryan Seacrest and company because, "Let's face it," Jackie said. "Ryan doesn't hold a candle to Dick." *Fair point*, I thought.

By the time we prepared all of the food, it was already after 10 pm. We sat around the table, discussing the past year and how we hoped 2023 would be less tumultuous than 2022. Actually, we hoped for less tumultuous than 2020, 2021, and 2022 since all three years had been brutal, what with the Covid 19 pandemic, a struggling economy, and the right-wing conservatives doing everything in their power to bring us back to 1950.

The conversation inevitably turned to resolutions, and we each had strong opinions about the subject.

"I never make them," Jackie said emphatically. "Why set yourself up for failure? Has anyone *ever* kept a resolution? By January tenth, they're ancient history."

"Oh, I don't know about that," Paige responded. "I think it's a good idea to set goals to kick off the year."

This piqued Kelly's interest. "So, what is the resolution for the new year, Paige?"

She looked at Jackie and smiled as she answered. "Maybe it's to be open to new possibilities."

Kelly rolled her eyes at them, and I laughed. "What's the matter, babe? You don't like that resolution?"

"I just think if you had asked Paige the same question a week ago, you'd have gotten a completely different answer."

Paige smiled at her sister, debating whether to challenge her or let it go. "So, what's your resolution, Kelly?"

"Surprisingly, I agree with Jackie. I don't make them."

"I do," I said. "And I rarely, if ever, verbalize them because then everyone knows if you've failed."

"Okay, so what was your 2022 resolution?" Kelly asked.

"Well...if I tell you, I will break my rule."

"What you really mean is if you tell us, our point will be proven because you didn't do it. Am I right, honey?"

I lowered my head, realizing she had me on this one. "Yes, but in my defense, I made it until March before I broke it."

Kelly laughed at me and grabbed my hand, bringing it to her lips for a conciliatory kiss. "What was it?"

"I resolved that we would have sex at least five times a week for the whole year."

Kelly scoffed at me. "Why would you make that resolution? We're way too old to keep up that pace."

"Speak for yourself," I said. "We're in our thirties. This is the prime of our sexual lives. I'll bet Jackie keeps up that pace!"

Jackie put her hands up in surrender, realizing there was no way to answer that without getting herself in trouble. "Hey, leave me out of this. Besides, you should never make resolutions involving sex. That's just a recipe for disaster. Sex needs to be spontaneous and spur of the moment, and fun. Planned sex is boring sex."

"Kelly, was sex with me at the beginning of this year boring?"

"Oh geez. This conversation has gone down quite a rabbit hole. Beth, my love, sex with you is never boring. Jackie, I agree. No resolutions should be made involving sex. And Paige, try not to be too open to new possibilities, okay? You make me nervous, especially since this one," she pointed to Jackie, "is involved. She'll take that as permission to lead you astray."

I looked at my wife rather indignantly since I was pretty certain she was placating me about sex and boredom. She picked up on my pouty face and tried to do damage control. "Babe, seriously. I'm not just saying that to shut you up, but really, five days a week for a whole year? You had to know we weren't going to make that one. Why did you feel the need to make a resolution out of it? Were we in a 'sexual drought' at the end of 2021?" She made air quotes as she said sexual drought.

"I remember that I had been reading a book last year about how to keep a marriage going strong. One of the tips was frequent sex, so I figured, well, that's a no-brainer. Happy marriage and more sex, right? Win-win. And by the way, we broke the streak only because I got the flu in March."

She smiled at me and leaned over for a kiss. "You're so cute, you know that?"

"What? Am I wrong? Unless you've been faking it, I'll go out on a limb and say you benefited from this resolution."

"Did you keep a log?" Jackie asked, making all three of them laugh at me.

"It's all up here." I pointed to my head. "Go ahead, laugh. But as far as I'm concerned, a resolution that encourages me to make love to my wife is a pretty good goal."

Paige looked at Jackie and said, "I think I might have to take a cue from Beth and make a 'have more sex' resolution."

Kelly rolled her eyes again and made a sound that could only be described as an emphatic scoff. She playfully smacked my arm and said, "Now look what you've done. We're going to need earplugs tonight. I'm not sure I can take listening to my baby sister having sex with your ex."

"We can always go back to the hotel if that's what you'd prefer, Kelly," Paige said. Jackie smiled at Paige and looked over to find Kelly shooting her a dirty look.

"No, no. You two can feel free to use our guest room to resolution yourselves to death as far as I'm concerned."

"Thank you. I think we will." Paige reached across the table to kiss Jackie.

"In the meantime, Beth and I will work on her 2023 resolution. So keep it down, okay?"

Chapter Nineteen

AFTER THE PEACH DROPPED at midnight (yes, they really do drop a peach in Atlanta in our lame attempt to compete with the ball dropping in Time Square), Kelly and I snuggled on the couch for a bit before heading to bed. My hopes for starting a new resolution faded quickly when I heard Kelly's breathing change into her adorable little snore that sounds a bit like a tree frog in the summertime. Meanwhile, from down the hall, it was obvious Paige and Jackie were not in the same boat. I decided to get Kelly up to bed before I heard too much. Listening to other people having sex gives me the willies. When I caressed her face to try to arouse her, she grunted at me, making it clear my efforts were not appreciated. I debated leaving her to sleep on the couch, weighing the possibility she would wake up and hear the sound of Jackie ravaging her little sister. I decided that was too risky, so I forced her to get up even though I had to suffer her crankiness all the way upstairs to the bedroom.

I sat her on the bed and took off her clothes, trying to get her into her pajamas. I finally decided it wasn't worth the trouble and swung her legs under the covers.

"What time is it?" she asked.

"A quarter to one. You must be getting old, babe. You barely made it to midnight."

"Just give me a minute to get my second wind, and we can start that New Year's resol..." She dozed off mid-sentence.

"It's okay, honey. Sleep well." I kissed her forehead, and she murmured something unintelligible. "I love you. Happy New Year."

* * * *

A few hours later, I was in the middle of a fabulous erotic dream when I realized it was real. My wife had her face nuzzled between my breasts, her hand finding its place between my legs. When she realized I was finally fully awake, she brought her lips up to mine and kissed me softly and slowly. "You didn't let me have my way with you before we went to bed," she said.

"The only thing you had your way with was your pillow, sweetheart. You were done for the night."

"Yeah, but I woke up so horny for you."

"I can see that. I can feel it too. I thought I was dreaming about you."

"Mmm. Can I have you?"

"Please do. I love it when you wake up like this." She disappeared under the covers, kissing me as she trailed down my stomach. I tilted my head back and closed my eyes, grateful we still felt such desire for each other after six years of marriage. 2023 was starting on the right foot.

* * * *

Jackie opened her eyes and peered at the clock on the nightstand. It was 8:00 AM, and she could smell coffee and bacon coming from the kitchen downstairs. She looked over to find the other side of the bed empty, and Paige was nowhere to be found. It occurred to her she missed Paige, which struck her as odd. On a typical morning after, Jackie was happy to wake up alone. It was always uncomfortable to slink away in the dark after one of her conquests or, worse, to ask them to leave her place soon afterward. For Jackie, it was always just about sex. Almost no kissing, no cuddling, and definitely no *sleeping* together. That was far too intimate. But for the past two nights, she had broken every one of those rules. She found the intimacy with Paige both thrilling and terrifying. She'd slept better than she had in years. And to wake up missing her? That was even more terrifying.

The bedroom door opened, and Paige appeared with a tray of food, juice, and coffee. She wore Jackie's tee shirt, and her shoulder-length hair was beautifully messy.

"Good morning," she said as she set the food tray on her side of the bed.

"Good morning. Why are you up so early?"

"It's eight o'clock. That's not early. I'm usually up by six. Besides, you were sleeping so soundly I didn't want to wake you. You snore, by the way."

"I do *not* snore."

"I beg to differ. I should have recorded it. I can't believe no one has ever told you that before."

"Well, at the risk of making myself look bad, I've instituted a pretty strict rule regarding sleeping with people. The rule is that I don't. So there've been very few people who have seen or heard me sleep."

"Ah, I see. So, given this rule, why is it I have woken up next to you for the past two mornings?"

"It's a valid question. I'm not sure I know the answer. But I've broken all of my rules with you for whatever reason."

"Are there more rules that I'm unaware of?"

Jackie sighed. Admitting this to Paige made her feel vulnerable. She took a sip of coffee and a bite of toast while formulating her response. "Several. Number one, I don't cuddle. And number two, I rarely kiss. Sometimes I don't even get naked, so I guess that's rule number three. Number four is the all-important 'no sleeping' rule."

Paige reached for Jackie's face, putting her finger under her chin to force their eyes to meet. "I feel honored. Scared but honored. We are four for four. Eat your eggs. They're going to get cold."

Jackie reached for her fork and did as she was told. "I'm glad I'm not the only one feeling frightened here. There's something about you, Paige. I haven't known you long enough yet to figure out what it is, but I hope I can get the opportunity to find out."

"I do, too," Paige said, leaning over to kiss her. "But we have a slight problem that will make that a bit difficult, don't you think?"

"What problem is that?"

"Well, I live in New York, and you live in D.C."

"What's a few hours up the Jersey Turnpike? Besides, I can run my business from anywhere. I only just moved to D.C. about a year ago. I needed to get out of Atlanta. A change of scenery was in order."

"Let me guess. Trouble with a woman?"

"You could say that." She sighed. "Every time I reveal some new tidbit of information about myself, I expect you to go running. Knowing what you know, why are you even interested in me? And believe me, you don't know the half of it. I think maybe your sister is right. You deserve better. You're way too good for me."

"My sister doesn't get to decide who I'm interested in. Maybe I see something in you that I like and want to explore. Is that so wrong?"

"No. I just think you might save yourself some trouble if you call this a 'holiday fling' and make your way back to New York unscathed."

"Jackie..."

"What?"

"I'm already scathed." Paige reached for the breakfast tray and moved it off the bed and onto the dresser. She returned to the bed and straddled her legs over Jackie's waist, leaning in to kiss her neck. "Do you really want me to make my way back to New York?" she whispered.

"No." Jackie's voice became breathy and soft, reacting to the feel of Paige's body on hers.

"Good," Paige said. "We have some more rules to break," she said as she reached for Jackie's tee shirt and pulled it over her head.

Chapter Twenty

THE MONDAY AFTER NEW Year's Day is always one of my least favorite days of the year. The holidays are over, and it's time to return to work. I woke up late and barked at Kelly, who was already in the shower, for not getting me up on time. She ignored me as usual, her way of reminding me I'm a big girl and should be responsible for my own wake-up time. I decided that since I was already late, I might as well take my time. No one in the office this early on January fifth would care if I was late, so I trotted down to the kitchen to ply myself with coffee.

I found Paige standing at the sink with a mug in one hand and a piece of coffee cake in the other. She stared out the window watching Ollie and Jake hunting squirrels in the yard.

"Why would anyone be up at this hour if they didn't have to go to work?" I asked.

"Isn't anyone here a morning person? It's daytime. There are things to do and people to see. I can't sleep my life away."

"It's a quarter after seven, Paige. I'd barely call that daytime."

"Well, it is for me. I've already been out for a run. It's beautiful outside."

I looked down at my Apple watch to see the temperature. "You and I have very different opinions, Paige. Forty-three degrees does not constitute beautiful."

"You've lived in the south for too long. A brisk morning run is the best way to start the day. Gets the heart going."

I scowled in obvious disdain. "Is Jackie still sleeping?"

"She was when I left her."

"Ah. So I take it you two are still cohabitating in our guest room?"

"Yep."

"Your sister is probably getting ready to bust from all the angst she is holding inside."

"She'll get over it."

"When do you plan to go back to New York?" I asked, wondering when we would have the house back to ourselves.

"I'm not sure. We don't have anyone booked in the studio until the end of the month, and my boss is currently in Bali." She must have seen the look of shock on my face. "Relax, Beth. I'm not staying that long."

"What? I didn't even say anything."

"The look on your face said it all."

"Are you playing it by ear to see where this thing goes with Jackie?"

"Maybe a little. I'm enjoying getting to know her. I hope the feeling is mutual."

"Well, considering she's still here after a week and a half, I think so. You have no idea how unusual that is. You've obviously cast some kind of spell over her."

Paige blushed a little and turned back toward the window. She saw the dogs sitting patiently by the door, so she let them in, and they came to greet me. Their tails whacked against the table legs, and they whimpered with excitement when I petted them.

"Do you think I'm crazy for getting involved with Jackie?" she asked me.

"Crazy? No. Impulsive? Maybe. Obviously, I get the appeal. Been there, done that, as they say. She can be very charming. And I have seen some personal growth from her on this trip, but I still think you should be cautious before you jump in."

Paige blushed again and smiled, telling me my advice was too late. "You've already jumped, haven't you?" I asked.

"Well, I'm trying to take it slow, but I don't think I'm succeeding. I think she's the one who has cast a spell on me because I'm finding it hard to keep my hands off her."

"Please don't tell Kelly that."

"Don't tell me what?" Kelly made her way into the kitchen. I was distracted by her appearance, looking very sexy in her work clothes.

"It's nothing, Kel. We were talking about Jackie, your favorite subject," Paige responded.

"Are you eloping with her or something?"

"Don't be ridiculous. We'll shack up long before we get married."

"Speaking of shacking up...how long do you two plan to continue fornicating in our guest room? I mean, it is January fifth. Don't you need to go back to work or something?"

"Geez, Kel. I'm surprised you don't have my bags packed and sitting by the front door. Beth, is she always this feisty first thing in the morning?" Paige seemed genuinely hurt by Kelly's apparent desire to have her leave. She put her coffee cup in the sink and made her way out of the kitchen when Kelly reached over to stop her.

"I'm sorry, Paige. I didn't really mean that. Well, maybe I did for Jackie, but not for you. You know you're always welcome here. My big sister instincts are kicking in because I know the longer you and Jackie continue this fling or whatever you want to call it, the harder it will be for you when it ends."

"Please stop trying to protect me, okay? I'm having fun. I'm enjoying myself. Can you let me have that please?"

Kelly pulled Paige into her arms for a bear hug. "You're right, and I'm sorry. I'll try to keep my reservations to myself."

"It would be even better if you allowed yourself to let those reservations go once and for all. Jackie might surprise you if you give her a chance."

"I suppose anything is possible. Okay, I'm late, and I have to get to work. Try not to have sex on every piece of furniture in the house while we're gone, okay?" She came over to kiss me goodbye, patted the dogs on their respective heads, and went out through the garage door.

"Your wife can be exasperating, you know that?"

"Don't blame me. She was your sister long before she became my wife."

Chapter Twenty-One

ABOUT AN HOUR AFTER Beth and Kelly left for work, Jackie finally made her way out of the bedroom, looking like she had slept for a month. The house was dead quiet, with the dogs lying in their beds, soaking up the morning sunshine beaming through the sliding glass door. Jake at least wagged his tail at her while Ollie just yawned and rolled over.

Jackie searched for Paige without success and asked the dogs where she went. She looked at them curiously, as if surprised that they hadn't answered her inquiry. As she pulled out her phone to text her, the front door opened, and Paige arrived with an armful of grocery bags. Her hair was tied back and tucked into her baseball cap, her face flushed from the cool, crisp January air. She wore her North Face jacket over her Lululemon workout gear.

"Good morning. You've slept half the day away." Paige made her way over to the kitchen counter to drop the bags, then turned to Jackie to give her a kiss.

"It's not even nine yet."

"For the second time today, I find myself asking—isn't anyone in this house a morning person?" Paige asked.

"What are you doing out so early?"

"I went to the market. I decided since Kelly and Beth had to return to work, you and I would spend the day in the kitchen baking breads and pies."

"The holidays are over. We should have done this a week ago."

"Yeah, well. Better late than never. I have a hankering for homemade bread, and the Granny Smith apples at the grocery store looked so perfect I couldn't resist. They're great for pies. I even got some fresh whipping cream and vanilla ice cream for pie a la mode. We can surprise our hostesses when they get home from work. The house will smell like baked goods, and we can indulge after dinner."

"I didn't know you were so domestic, Paige."

Paige walked over to Jackie, kissed her, and said, "There's a lot you don't know about me. This is just one of my many talents." She turned and started opening cabinet doors, looking for the appropriate baking supplies. Then she connected her phone to the Bluetooth speaker and streamed her favorite station, the one that played every genre of music.

After an hour of preparation, the bread dough was set aside to rise, and Paige turned to the pie-making process. Jackie sat at the table and watched during the bread-making because that was a one-person job, but Paige signaled for Jackie to join her at the counter while they cleaned, peeled, and cut the apples. Jackie would peel one, then eat one, peel one, then eat one. Eventually, Paige sent her back to the table, worried they would run out of apples if she kept going at that pace.

Instead of returning to her seat, she took the knife from Paige, put it on the counter, then spun her around into her arms to dance with her to *Unchained Melody* by the Righteous Brothers. Paige resisted at first, complaining her hands were full of apple. Jackie ignored her and brought her close, moving together with her to the beat.

"Remember the movie *Ghost*, and there was the scene with this song playing while Demi Moore worked the pottery wheel? God, that was so sexy. I had such a crush on her," Paige confessed.

"You were a baby when that movie came out!"

"Well, obviously I didn't see it until I was older. I remember being about seventeen when I first saw it. I wanted to get a pottery wheel just so my girlfriend and I could fool around while playing with the clay."

"Was this your first love?"

"Yes," Paige said, pulling away from their embrace.

"What was her name?" Jackie asked.

"Lori. Her name was Lori." Paige put her head down and went back to cutting apples.

"Did I bring up a sore subject?" Jackie asked.

"It's okay." Paige turned away, pretending to look for something in the cabinet. Jackie came up behind her and reached for her.

"Hey, talk to me. What just happened? If I did something to upset you, I apologize. What is it?"

"Let's just finish the pie, okay?" She changed the station on the Bluetooth to something more upbeat, and she continued with her preparations. Jackie dropped it for the moment, giving Paige a chance to finish her task. She could tell there was a story there, but the timing was off, so she decided to wait until they could sit and talk it out with undivided attention.

Paige quietly went about the process of making the crust, filling the pie pan, and preparing it to bake. She moved about the kitchen robotically and sullenly. The conversation and light-hearted mood from earlier had vanished, and Jackie felt responsible for ruining their day.

Once the pie and the bread were in the oven, and the kitchen was cleaned, Jackie took Paige's hand and led her into the living room. Paige went to turn on the television, but Jackie reached for the remote and stopped her. They sat down facing each other, Jackie on the sofa and Paige in the armchair. Jackie grabbed her hands and brought them to her lips, kissing them softly.

"Paige, please. Talk to me. It's obvious that whatever memory I triggered in there was a bad one. Won't you tell me about it?"

"It's not your fault. Really, it's fine. It's ancient history."

"Tell me about Lori. Please?"

Paige sighed and lowered her head. Jackie could see the tears had already started to roll down her cheeks, so she reached over to wipe them away with her thumb.

"It's not a happy story."

"I kind of figured that."

"But what if I don't want you to see my bad stuff yet?"

"Why not?"

"Because we're in the having fun stage. Heavy stuff is reserved for down the road *if* the relationship gets that far. I know we aren't in that place. I don't want you to feel like you need to deal with it."

"Are you afraid I'll hear your sad story, get bummed out, and take a hike?"

"I don't know. Maybe."

"I'm not quite that shallow, all evidence to the contrary. If I recall, I said I wanted to get to know you. Did you think I meant only the fun stuff?"

"I don't know. Maybe."

"Do you want to know only the fun stuff about me?"

"No. I want to know everything."

"Okay then. Can you extend the same courtesy to me, please? Look, Paige. I'm not going to lie. You scare the shit out of me. Want to know why?"

"Yes."

"I woke up this morning, and you were gone from the bed. I came out here, and I couldn't find you. I looked out front, and your car wasn't there. And I thought, 'Well. That's it. She took off. She's done with me.' The feeling of sadness that overcame me was so strong. I can't remember the last time I felt that. I'm not sure I ever felt it, to be honest. Maybe a little with Beth, but not like this. You've got me all twisted up inside. I'm not sure how this is possible after such a short time, but that's a conversation for another day.

"My point is that I'm not just here for fun. If you've got something heavy weighing on your mind, I want to hear it, and I want to see if I can help. And if I can't, then I can at least listen and let you get it off your chest."

Paige dropped Jackie's hands, wiped her eyes, and stood up. She went into the kitchen, pretending to check the oven. Jackie knew she was stalling, but she just waited until Paige was ready. When she returned to the living room, she sat on the floor next to Ollie. As she petted him, she sighed, looked up at Jackie, and started to speak.

Chapter Twenty-Two

2006

PAIGE SAT ACROSS FROM Lori at the Outback Steakhouse and dredged her wedge of Blooming Onion into the dipping sauce. Lori mindlessly did the same while browsing real estate listings on her Blackberry.

"There's a two-bedroom loft about a mile from campus," she told Paige.

"Two bedrooms in midtown Atlanta? That probably costs a fortune. What's the rent?"

"It doesn't say, but it does describe it as reasonable."

"Call the number. I'll bet you it's at least twelve hundred dollars a month. We don't have that kind of money, Lori. A thousand dollars is our upper limit, and even that's a bit too high. My class load this semester is going to be crazy, and I won't have any extra time to get another job. And you're in the same boat since you'll be working in the Engineering lab whenever you have a spare minute."

"My mom said she would help me with the rent."

"Yeah—help. Not pay it. I don't want you spending every waking hour that you don't have class at work. We'll never see each other. I'd rather live in a dump and be able to spend more time with you."

"We could get a roommate."

"No! No roommates. I want you all to myself. I don't want to worry that someone else will come walking in when I'm having my way with you on the kitchen counter."

"The kitchen counter, huh? Won't that be kind of uncomfortable?"

"Okay, the floor. Or the couch. Or the shower. Wherever we see fit."

"It's going to be so nice when we don't have to sneak around our parents to find time to be together. If my parents only knew how often we've done it in my little twin bed."

"The first thing we are buying is a queen-sized bed!" Paige said excitedly.

Lori dialed the number for the loft while they waited for their food to come. She talked to the leasing agent and asked multiple questions about rent, utilities, amenities, and distance from Georgia Tech. Paige was shocked she hadn't hung up as soon as Lori asked about the rent, but Lori could talk to anyone about anything, so she just figured she was making polite conversation.

When she hung up, she said, "Well, we're in luck! It's one thousand fifty dollars a month. I made an appointment to see it tomorrow."

"Lori, we just talked about this! That's over our limit."

"Oh, please. Fifty dollars over. That doesn't even count. I'm sure we spend that on takeout food in a month. We'll be better about cooking for ourselves instead. C'mon, please, Paige? Let's at least go see it, okay?"

"Fine. We'll look. No promises, though. What time is the appointment?"

"Three o'clock. I'll meet you there since I have to work until two-thirty."

After indulging in their cheeseburgers at Outback, they got back to Paige's house to find they were alone, with Paige's parents out at a movie and her sister Kelly away at the University of Georgia. They were met at the door by Chico, Paige's Yorkshire terrier. Paige put his leash on him, and they walked him down the street. The summer heat felt oppressive as they held hands and strolled into the neighborhood park. Chico sniffed around for his perfect spot while they chatted.

"Do you think our parents will have a hard time once they find out we're together?" Lori asked.

"I doubt it. They know my sister is gay, and they don't have any problems with it. My parents should be fine. I can't speak for yours."

"I think they might be more challenging. They love you, but that's because they don't know you're fucking their baby girl."

"You have such a delicate way with words, Lor."

"I speak the truth. Are you not fucking me?"

"Yes, I am, but I prefer to say 'I make love to you.'" Paige laughed as she said it, and Lori joined in.

"You're so corny, but okay, yes. Sometimes, you make love to me, but others, you definitely fuck me."

"That is very true," Paige responded and pulled Lori in for a kiss. "What would you prefer tonight, baby? Do you want to make love, or do you want to fuck? My parents won't be home for at least a few more hours. You decide."

"Hmmm. That's a tough choice. I like it both ways, but since I'm feeling sentimental about us living together, I choose your tender side, please."

When they arrived back at the house, Paige gave Chico his treat, and he trotted off to his bed to eat it in peace. As Paige put away the leash and harness, Lori came up behind her and kissed the back of her neck. She put her arms around Paige's waist and spun her around, finding her lips and kissing them passionately. Paige put her hands on Lori's face, cupping her cheeks as she pulled her in close. "Babe, I love you so much," Paige whispered. "Soon, we'll be able to do this every night. I can't wait to start my life with you."

Lori's breathing was labored, and Paige could feel her getting worked up. "Start *now*, baby. I need you." Lori's hands trailed down to Paige's ass, and she pulled her hips into her. Paige reached for her button fly and pulled, releasing some of the pressure. She moved away momentarily, looked Lori in the eyes, then grabbed her hand and led her down the hall to Paige's bedroom. She closed and locked the door and found Lori undressing when she turned back toward her.

Paige made her way across the room to help her pull off her jeans. She sat Lori down on the bed and made her wait while Paige took off her clothes slowly and deliberately in her own version of a striptease. Lori groaned in anticipation.

"Patience." When Paige was finally ready, she pushed Lori back onto the bed and put her body down on top of her, skin to skin from head to toe. "You are so beautiful. Do you know that?" She ran her hands over Lori's breasts with a tantalizing touch.

Lori's eyes met hers as she answered, "You're biased. I'm only beautiful because you love me."

"Not true. Just look at you. Is there anything more perfect than this body, this face, this heart?"

"Are you going to talk, or are you going to take me?"

"You said you wanted to make love," Paige said.

"I do, but if you're going to drive me crazy, I will change my vote. I'm going to come without you even touching me."

"No, you won't. I'll make sure of that." She pulled her hands off and lowered her face to kiss her lightly. Lori reached in to pull her close, but Paige resisted, making her wait. She stared into Lori's eyes and said, "Am I worth waiting for, baby?"

"Of course you are," Lori responded breathlessly.

"Tell me what you want me to do to you." Paige lowered her head to Lori's breast and blew lightly on the tip of her nipple. "Do you want more of this?"

"Yes...please." Paige obliged and put her lips on her breast, sucking them slowly.

Paige took Lori's hand and put it between Lori's legs, letting her feel just how excited she was. "Do you want me to touch you there?"

"Yes...please, Paige."

Paige pushed her fingers in just far enough to elicit a sound from her, and then she pulled them out again. She brought her fingers up to her mouth, tasting her wetness. "Oh my god," Paige said. "You are so perfect. I want you more right now than I ever have before." She leaned over Lori's body and maneuvered herself down toward her belly, kissing her stomach while stroking her breasts. Lori's breathing was the only sound in the room, growing increasingly labored.

"I need you..."

Paige dove her tongue in between Lori's legs. Paige slowly and rhythmically rode the waves of Lori's movements, bringing her to the brink, then pulling her back again. Lori cried out as the rush of emotions flooded the space between them. Paige watched, listened, and felt Lori's body going through its motions of ecstasy. Lori screamed Paige's name and pulled away from her, the intensity too great to handle. Gasping for breath, she pulled Paige down on top of her, and they lay together in recovery, skin to skin from head to toe.

* * * *

Paige arrived at the apartment building at 2:45, meeting the landlord in the lobby. They were going to wait for Lori before going up to the loft, but he decided to take Paige up first to give her more time to look around.

He gave her the history of the building, a renovated industrial space that used to house a clothing factory in the 1940s. It was a beautiful open space, with tall windows bringing in the afternoon sunlight. Paige imagined the rows and rows of seamstresses at their Singer sewing machines, gazing out those windows and waiting for their workday to be done. The exposed piping was a nice touch, although Paige was concerned it would be hard to keep the space cool with the high ceilings.

The kitchen had been remodeled, and Paige could see herself cooking dinner while Lori did her homework in the huge living room. She walked around, feeling the energy of the room and realizing she had already fallen in love with it without even trying. Lori would be saying 'I told you so' any minute now.

She went into the bedroom to find even more large industrial windows. The closets were on the small side, but they could make it work. She went to the windows to see the view, finding the faint outline of Stone Mountain in the distance to the east. This room would get its sunlight in the morning, and she imagined the rays of light coming across their bed as they awoke. She looked down at the street below to see the afternoon rush hour traffic making its way over to Interstate 75/85, just a block or so away.

The horns from the street below caught her attention, and Paige smiled when she looked down to find Lori getting ready to cross the road to get to the building. As Lori waited for the light to change, the sound of screeching brakes, so loud Paige could hear them from three floors up, and then a crash as a moving van barreled into the sidewalk, taking everything in its path as it careened into the convenience store on the corner.

Paige watched in horror, then screamed so loudly the landlord came running into the room to see what was wrong. Paige ran out of the building, crying out as she descended the stairs. By the time she made it to the scene of the accident, bystanders were trying to help the injured. Paige scanned the scene for Lori but couldn't find her. Multiple people were on the ground, bleeding and screaming out in pain. For a moment, she thought maybe Lori got out of the way in time and had moved down the street away from the chaos. As she turned to look, she saw the wheels of the van, mangled and twisted. Underneath the tire, she could see Lori's well-worn Doc Marten shoes.

With adrenaline-fueled intensity, she grabbed the mangled metal, lifting it as if her life depended on it. Many bystanders joined her when they realized Lori was beneath the tire. Together, they managed to lift just enough weight off to drag Lori out from beneath the twisted rubber tire. Paige called her name, desperately hoping to get a response. She put her ear to Lori's face, listening for signs of life. She begged Lori to respond. As she started to give CPR, she put her hands on Lori's chest, preparing to administer compressions. Her rib cage was completely flattened, with bones protruding and blood pouring out faster than Paige could contain it.

The paramedics arrived and forcibly pushed Paige out of the way. She screamed as they held her back. One of the police officers on the scene pulled her about ten feet away toward his patrol car.

"That's my girlfriend!" Paige screamed. "Please, let me go. I have to be with her!"

"Okay, miss, okay! Just give the paramedics a chance to do their jobs. They need room to work. I'll let you over there as soon as I can."

Paige continued to scuffle with him. "Miss, please! Listen, just take a breath. I need you to calm down. Tell me her name."

"Lori Stewart," Paige said breathlessly.

"Okay, good. How old is she?"

"She's eighteen." Paige struggled for air as if hyperventilating.

"How long have you been together?"

"Two years."

"You two are young to have been together so long," the officer said, speaking calmly in a futile attempt to get Paige to stop fighting him to get to Lori.

"I love her. I'm going to marry her." Paige craned her neck, watching the paramedics apply CPR repeatedly, shocking her with their portable defibrillator.

"She's a lucky girl. What's your name?"

"Paige. Paige Gallagher. Officer, please. I've got to be with her. I have to tell her I'm here!"

The officer glanced over to the paramedic performing CPR, who shook his head, signaling that it was a fruitless attempt. He hesitated for a moment, then let go of Paige to let her rush to Lori's side.

"Lor. Lori! Listen to me!" Paige lowered her face to Lori's, the tears dripping down onto her bloodied cheeks. "You can't leave me! No, this can't be happening. No!" She screamed as the paramedic stopped doing compressions on her chest. She fell into Lori's lifeless body and stayed there, whispering in Lori's ear until the officer and the paramedic lifted her by the arms and took her away.

Chapter Twenty-Three

2006

KELLY WALKED INTO THE church, holding her sister's hand and guiding her to the second pew behind Lori's parents. Paige moved robotically, going where Kelly directed her to go. She had hardly spoken a word since the day began. The church was crowded with family and friends, but Paige had ignored them all as they moved down the aisle. Her eyes were focused on the coffin in front of the altar.

It was incomprehensible that her future rested inside that wood structure, never to be able to share in the life they had imagined for themselves. Paige was going to propose as soon as they had moved in together. She had been saving money and wanted to take Lori on their honeymoon to Aruba because Lori had said she'd always wanted to go there. Lori was going to be a chemical engineer, while Paige would study biochemistry with hopes of doing research for the CDC in Atlanta. Those plans died on the pavement at the corner of Techwood and Tenth Street.

After the burial, Kelly guided Paige into their parent's house, where family and friends were set to gather. Kelly knew Paige would not be able to handle the crowd, so she led her directly to her bedroom and closed the door behind them. Paige sat on the bed, and Kelly removed her black suit jacket and hung it on the back of her desk chair.

"Can I get you some water, Paige?"

She shook her head no. She hadn't uttered a word in the three hours since the limo had picked them up that morning.

"Do you want to lie down? I can help you out of this suit and into something more comfortable."

Another head shake.

"Paige, I don't know how to help you through this. What can I do?"

Paige looked at her as the tears rolled down her cheeks. "I think I need to move out of this house," she said. "I can't sleep in this room—in this bed. Do you know how many times Lori and I made love in this bed? How many times I told her how much I loved her? We used to complain about how small it was. I laughed and said she never gave me any room, but the truth is, I couldn't get close enough. It's like I wanted to be inside her—in her heart and her body. I can't sleep here anymore."

"You'll come live with me in my apartment at UGA."

"Maybe for a little while, but not permanently. Your future is still ahead of you, and you don't need me getting in the way. My future just died, in every sense of that word."

"Let's take this one day at a time, okay? I'm not going to sit here and offer you platitudes that are meaningless to you right now. All you need to do at this moment is get through to the next moment and the next after that. None of us are going to tell you how to grieve. We'll be here for you and hold your hand. Well, we might make sure you occasionally eat, too, but otherwise, you'll deal with this as you see fit."

"I want to die, Kel."

"No. I'm not going to let you do that."

"You just said you would let me deal with it as I want. Well, I want to die. I can't do this. I'm not strong enough. I want to be with her."

"There is no way Lori would want that for you. I'm sure of it. And you have no idea just how strong you truly are." She knelt in front of Paige and grabbed her hands. "Listen. This is the absolute worst that life has to offer. You will probably never feel the depth of despair you are feeling right now. There is nowhere to go but up. My goal is to get you through these first few weeks. We'll figure out what comes next after that, okay?"

Paige nodded, too spent to argue with her sister. Kelly took her hand and led her out the door and into Kelly's old room. She helped her out of her suit, gave her an old T-shirt and a pair of sweats, and guided her into Kelly's bed. She pulled the covers up, kissed her forehead, and closed the blinds, shielding her from the bright sunshine.

"I love you, Paige. Get some rest. I'm here if you need me."

She left the room and closed the door behind her.

Chapter Twenty-Four

JACKIE WAITED FOR A cue from Paige that her story was finished. She had been sitting on the edge of the sofa, listening intently, crying occasionally, and reaching for Paige's hand when she thought additional comfort would be welcomed. Now that Paige seemed to have said all she was going to say, Jackie sat back and took a deep breath. Paige got up from the floor and went to the kitchen.

"I'm getting a Coke. Would you like one?" she asked.

"No, thank you. I...uh, I need a min..." Paige came back in and sat across from Jackie on the chair.

"Jackie, it's okay. I'm okay. It was a long time ago."

"I'm going to take a guess and say that this is something you probably don't just get over, Paige. It's no wonder it hits you sideways sometimes. I...I can't even imagine what that must have been like for you. To experience that kind of heartbreak at such a young age. To be honest, I'm shocked you're as well-adjusted as you are after that."

"It took a long time. A very long time. And Kelly made sure I stuck it out. Believe me, there were times those first few months when I wasn't so sure, but she kept me going. I owe a lot to my sister, which is why her opinion is so important to me. And it's also why she's so protective of me."

"Then why are you involved with me, given how she feels about me?"

"Because you're the first person I've wanted to get to know since Lori. Sure, there've been women here and there, but none I would stick around for. The minute I met you, I saw something in you I needed to explore. So, as much as I hate disappointing her, I've reached a point in my life where I need to go with my gut." Jackie smiled and leaned over to kiss her softly. "And listen, I'm sorry I freaked out earlier when you asked me about Lori. As you said, it just hits me sometimes, but after all this time, I get past it pretty quickly."

"You don't need to apologize to me. I'm grateful you told me. I feel privileged you think you can trust me enough to talk to me about it."

"Maybe someday, if whatever this thing is between us lasts, you'll tell me your deep dark secrets."

"How do you know I have any?"

Paige laughed. "I'm certain of it. You have all the signs."

"Oh, really? And what are those signs?"

"Let's see. Fear of commitment, sleeping around, never getting too close, sabotaging relationships. Shall I keep going?"

"No. I've heard enough, thanks."

"When you're ready to tell me about the source of all these things, I'm here to listen. In the meantime, I don't want to dwell on this story or this mood, okay? Let's finish our baking, and then maybe we can find a way to pass the time for the rest of the day."

She climbed into Jackie's lap on the sofa and kissed her. Jackie understood the hint, but tempered her reaction, still reeling from the story Paige had told her. Instead of intensifying the kiss, she pulled Paige's head down to rest on her chest, holding her there while they both got lost in their thoughts. After watching Paige relive the worst moment of her life, it felt disrespectful for Jackie to do anything other than hold her. So instead, she just sat in the moment with Paige, caressing her hair and listening to her breathing.

Chapter Twenty-Five

I CAME HOME FROM work that day to find the house smelling of freshly baked bread. As I entered the kitchen, I saw two whole loaves and one half-eaten loaf, along with a beautiful apple pie on its cooling tray. Knowing my wife and her limited baking skills, and considering that I watched her leave for work earlier that morning, I knew it had to be Paige's doing.

I took a piece from the partially eaten loaf and looked to the heavens to thank whatever god may have given Paige her ability to create such a wonderful indulgence. I went looking for her to thank her, only to find her and Jackie asleep in each other's arms on the couch. I tiptoed out of the room, but Jake decided to shake as he got up off his bed to greet me, and the clanging of his tags woke Jackie.

She disengaged herself from Paige's embrace without waking her, a skill I was confident she had honed over the years, leaving stealthily in the middle of the night. She met me in the kitchen, and we both took another piece of bread.

"I see Paige was productive today. Did you assist? This is delicious."

"I handed her stuff and turned on the oven." I laughed at her answer. At least she was honest and didn't try to inflate her role in the process.

"Looks like you two were having a lovely nap. Baking is hard work, I guess. Did you defile my couch before you fell asleep?"

"You have a one-track mind, Beth. No, we did not. We had kind of an emotional afternoon, so sex seemed like a bad idea."

"What happened?"

"She told me about Lori. The whole story. It was...heartbreaking. I don't know how she managed to get through it."

"One day at a time, from what Kelly has told me."

"Yeah, that's what she said as well. It sounds like she's only alive today thanks to Kelly. And now I understand Kelly's reactions a whole lot better. If I were her, I wouldn't trust me either." As she finished this sentence, Kelly walked in from the garage and heard her name.

"My reaction to what?" she asked. "Regardless of the topic, though, it's true. I don't trust you."

"I know. And now I know why, besides the obvious from my reputation."

"What do you mean? Did something happen today?"

"Paige told me about Lori."

"I see," Kelly said cautiously.

"I...she just...um, I had no idea. I still can't shake it, to be perfectly honest."

"Yeah, well, it's not an easy thing to shake. Is she okay? Where is she?"

"She's asleep on the couch."

"No, I'm not," we heard from the living room. "You all talk really loudly." Paige came walking into the kitchen, her hair standing on end from sleeping on it. "It's okay, everyone. Yes, I told Jackie about Lori. I'm fine. She's fine. We're all fine, okay?"

I was skeptical, but took her word for it. Kelly, on the other hand, was less inclined to believe her. "You always say you're fine, and you don't let yourself feel whatever you're feeling."

"Kel, I've been feeling this for sixteen years. Trust me. I'm not holding anything in. It came up in conversation today, and I wanted to tell Jackie about it. I'm not going to fall apart again. I've finally reached the point where I can think about it without becoming catatonic. And even though I'm sure you don't want to hear this, I feel close enough to Jackie now to trust her with this. As you know, I don't just blurt out this story to anyone."

"I know, I know," Kelly said.

I could tell this was the point that was bothering her. Paige was falling for Jackie. Otherwise, she'd never have discussed this with her. Kelly would have to accept this relationship whether she wanted to or not, because I got the feeling it was getting serious already. I just hoped Jackie had it in her to be careful with Paige's heart. It may have mended, but the cracks were still there below the surface.

Chapter Twenty-Six

JACKIE COULDN'T SLEEP. SHE stared at the ceiling and listened to Paige's rhythmic breathing. It was too warm in their room. Paige was always cold, so she had cranked the heat before coming to bed. She was bundled in long sleeve pajamas, whereas Jackie was naked and feeling very overheated. She turned on her side to look at Paige, watching her eyes flitting about in their REM stage. She wanted to reach over and caress her, but the fear of waking her held her back. So instead, she stared at this woman who had so drastically impacted Jackie's thought process in just a few short weeks.

She was supposed to go back to D.C. at the end of December. Now, it was mid-January, and the thought of leaving Paige made her feel physically ill. It occurred to her that at thirty-five years old, this was the first time she felt like she was truly in love. She'd had glimpses of it over the years. Beth was one of those glimpses, but this was different. Scary. Wonderful, but scary. She had come to the realization in the shower the morning after Paige had told her about Lori.

She rehashed their conversation in her head as the water was spilling down on her. Typically, when a woman she was with got too close or too personal, her instinct was to take off, the sooner, the better. With Paige, she felt the need to do exactly the opposite. She wanted to stay. She wanted to try to fill the hole in Paige's heart. She could never replace Lori, but she could help Paige start chapter two. As she was drying herself off in the shower, she realized the only explanation for this feeling was love. And even though it terrified her, she wanted to go with it instead of fighting it and running away.

She took her finger and very lightly ran it down Paige's side, from her breast to her hip. Paige moved but didn't wake up. She slid her finger under Paige's long-sleeved shirt to feel her skin. She wanted more, but Paige looked so peaceful, and she didn't want to disturb her. Maybe she was in the middle of a good dream. Her fingers ran up and down her side very softly until she could no longer resist, and she moved her hand onto Paige's breast. She still didn't wake up. Jackie whispered close to her.

"Paige, honey. Can you hear me?" When there was still no movement, Jackie leaned in closer and said, "My sweet Paige. What have you done to me? I love you. I never thought I'd say those words, but it's true. I'm in love with you."

Jackie decided not to push her luck and laid down on her back, letting out a deep sigh. She rolled over away from Paige to try to fall back to sleep. Within a few seconds, Paige was spooning her, nuzzling into the back of her neck.

"I love you too, Jack."

Jackie spun around and faced her. "You pretended to be asleep?"

"No, not really. I was in that half asleep, half awake phase. I felt you touching me, but I thought I was dreaming it. When you started talking, that's when I came out of it. I wanted to hear what you had to say. I'm glad I did." She smiled and kissed Jackie, putting her hand on her cheek. "Do you really think you're in love with me?"

"I don't think it. I know it. I love you, Paige. I don't know how this happened. And I don't know what we're going to do about it, but here we are."

"You know," Paige said in a whisper, "I've held my heart at bay for a long, long time. I've avoided anything other than a casual fling here and there. I thought I would continue that for the rest of my life because it was easier that way, but the minute I met you, I knew there was something different. I surprised myself by letting it happen instead of turning my back on it like I've done so many times before."

"Do you want to try to make this work, Paige?"

"I do. Do you?"

"Yes, but I'm *so* afraid I'm going to fuck it up."

"How about we put our efforts into making it work instead of worrying about fucking it up, okay? I think our bigger problem is that we live a few hundred miles away from each other."

"We can figure that out. Planes, trains, and automobiles. The only thing I know for sure right now is that I'm not ready for this to end. I want to be with you, to learn more about you every day. When I look ahead to the next phase of my life, I see you in it. That's never happened to me before."

Paige leaned in and kissed her. "So I'm the lucky girl who gets to tame the wild Jackie Fairburn, huh?"

"I'm not sure I would call it luck. Remember, I'm a handful. I get in my own way. I have a fear of commitment. I sleep around. I never get too close. And I sabotage relationships."

Paige cringed. "Ouch. You're using my own words against me."

"Well, you're not wrong."

"That may be true, but I think I'm right about this. If you didn't want to be here right now, in my bed, in my life, in my heart...you'd be long gone."

"*That* is very true."

"So if you want to be here, you must feel something different. And different feelings can result in different actions."

"Hmmm...those are pretty wise words for one forty-five in the morning. I'm impressed."

"Don't be. Maybe it's the ramblings of an exhausted mind."

"Maybe, but since I like what you're saying, I'm sticking with impressed." Jackie put her fingers on Paige's lips and traced their outline. "You know I have to go home soon."

"I know. So do I. My boss returns in a couple of days, and I have to get back to work."

"So how do we do this once we leave this little bubble we've been in?" Jackie asked.

"One day at a time. We'll FaceTime. I'll come down. You'll come up."

"If I leave the day after tomorrow, I can be back in time to meet this client that could bring in big money for the business. Are you okay with that?"

"I will miss you, but yes. Much as I'd like to spend our days talking, making love, and sleeping, the real world beckons. We'll be okay. I trust you."

"You do?"

"Yes, I do."

"I'm not sure anyone has ever said that to me. I'm going to do everything I can to not let you down, Paige. I don't want to be with anybody else. I won't be."

"I know."

Paige realized Jackie had tears running down her cheeks, and she wiped them away with her thumbs. She kissed Jackie softly, then opened her mouth to let her tongue glide across Jackie's lips. Jackie reached for her and pulled her in close, running her hands down her back. Paige murmured as Jackie kissed her neck while her hands continued to explore up and down her body.

She pulled the heavy pajamas over Paige's head, then tugged and wrestled with her pants until they were finally kicked to the floor. Paige spread her legs apart and let Jackie in, figuratively and literally. They moved in sync with each other, pulling, pushing, giving, and taking pleasure until their strength was depleted. Then they fell asleep in each other's arms, whispering I love you as they drifted off.

* * * *

In mid-January, Jackie announced it was time for her to get back to her business, at least for a little while. I was glad she had waited a few days after Paige's revealing story, because I didn't want it to look like she was taking off *because* of what Paige had told her.

It occurred to me that the old Jackie might have decided she was more likely than not to hurt Paige, and she might as well split before she got in too deep. That would not have gone over well, especially with Kelly. I'd heard Paige say she had no expectations and would be fine if it didn't work out. It was probably true, but Kelly sure wasn't going to see it that way.

We all had dinner together the night before Jackie was set to head back to D.C. Everyone seemed upbeat, but I could read the subtle undertone at the table. Paige wanted her to stay, and shockingly, deep down, I could tell Jackie wanted to do just that. I felt bad for both of them, but truthfully, it was never the plan for them to move in, and they had pretty much done just that in these last few weeks. It was time to get back to real life so we could all figure out what happened next. For Kelly and I, we needed to get our house back. For Paige and Jackie, they needed to find out if the long-distance thing was viable.

Kelly decided to play the big sister role, and she broached the subject. "So, what comes next for you, Jackie?"

"Well, I've got a few things I need to handle at home. We've got some important clients coming to town, and I have to be there to iron out a few potential consulting contracts."

"What about you and my sister?"

Paige chimed in. "Uh, hello! Your sister is sitting right here, Kel. I think that's probably a conversation Jackie and I need to have alone."

"Well, have you?" Kelly asked. I started to get nervous because I could see Paige's hackles going up.

"Actually, we have," Paige said. She looked at Jackie as if to ask permission to reveal their plans. Jackie nodded in agreement. "We're going to give the long-distance thing a try. We've agreed not to see other people and to trust each other."

Kelly lowered her head and whispered something under her breath. *Uh-oh*, I thought. That wasn't going to go over very well.

"Kel, would you like to say something?"

"I said, 'good luck with that.'" Yep, I was right. Paige made a sound of derision and stood up to leave the room. I looked over at Kelly, giving her a look and waiting to see if she was going to apologize. When it didn't seem likely, I decided to offer my opinion.

"Paige, wait. Don't be like that." I got up and gently tugged at her arm to keep her from leaving. "You know Kelly is always on the defensive where you're concerned." Kelly started to object, but I put my hand up to stop her before she said anything else she might come to regret later. "I think I know your sister pretty well, and I know exactly what she's thinking." Again, I put up my hand to keep Kelly from interjecting. "Babe, I can see by the look on your face that you don't have anything good to say, but you want to speak anyway. You and I both know that's a mistake." Kelly lowered her head just enough to let me know she was inclined to agree with me. Instead of fighting me, she stood up and got herself a beer from the fridge.

"Paige, look at this from Kelly's perspective. You recently shared with us that you've told Jackie about Lori. We know you. Kelly knows you better than anyone in the world. If you've shared this with Jackie, it's a sign you're getting serious. You're opening up your heart, which, in case anyone is interested in *my* opinion, is a good thing. So, imagine if the roles were reversed and you were the one who had picked Kelly up off the floor, literally. You were the one who made sure she kept breathing. Wouldn't you be terrified the next time she fell? You can't be with her all the time, right? So how do you know she'll be okay if she falls? She tells you she's strong, but that doesn't make it any easier. She was always strong, even before she fell." I watched Kelly out of the corner of my eye and realized her eyes were tearing. I kept going.

"Let's take this scenario one step further. What if Kelly was with me, but I had a bad habit of tripping the person I was with? How would that add to your stress?"

Jackie butted in. "Hey, can we not make me out to be abusive in this little picture you're painting?"

"Relax, Jackie. It's a metaphor. No one thinks you're abusive."

Paige walked over to where Kelly was leaning against the counter. I expected her usual response to Kelly—the 'I'm a big girl' and 'you don't need to protect me'—but she proved me wrong.

"Thank you, Kelly. I love you for picking me up off the floor. If Beth ever trips you, I'll be right there to return the favor."

Paige put her arms around Kelly, leaving it at that. Kelly hugged her tightly, and Jackie and I smiled at each other. They held each other for a long time, and I imagined both were somewhat lost in the memory of that tragedy long ago. I could hear faint sounds of sniffling, and Kelly broke the embrace to reach for a tissue. She came over to me and hugged me, her way of thanking me for preventing an argument that would've been just another rehash of every other skirmish these two sisters had this month.

Paige went back to her seat and skooched over closer to Jackie. She took her hand and then made another announcement to us.

"I'm leaving tomorrow as well, guys. I've got to get back to work. You're finally going to be rid of us. And I'm sorry we stayed so much longer than we expected." She looked into Jackie's eyes and smiled. "I guess when you come across something worth sticking around for, it's hard to walk away."

"Except that, as we said earlier, we're not walking away from each other," Jackie proclaimed. "I really want to give this a shot." Jackie stood and walked over to Kelly. "I think it's been well established on this trip that I am not to be trusted, and everyone is scared for Paige. I get it. But I want to say something."

She grabbed each of Kelly's hands in hers and faced her eye to eye. "I don't say this for any reason other than it's the truth. I'm not looking for sympathy or attention. I just want this to be known. Kelly, I'm scared too. And this will sound shitty, but I'm scared for myself. Do you know why? It's because I've *never* felt this way before. My heart has never been broken because I've never invested enough to let that happen. And for the record, Beth, I regret that I didn't invest it in you, but that ship has sailed, and I think we can all agree it all worked out for the best.

"But with Paige...it's different. My heart is out there on a ledge without any safety ropes, and I am terrified." She swallowed hard and dropped one of Kelly's hands so she could turn sideways to look at Paige. "I'm in love with her, Kelly. I know it's fast, and I'm a flight risk, but the way I feel at the thought of leaving her tomorrow makes me want to figure out how to make this work because I don't want to be without her." She walked over to Paige and put her hands on her cheeks, kissing her softly. "I don't want to be without you, Paige."

Kelly sighed as if acknowledging she'd been beaten. If she objected now, it would just make her look bitter. She watched as Paige and Jackie kissed, letting a hint of a smile cross her lips. Maybe it was time to loosen the reins a bit. Paige looked happy, so Kelly had decided in that moment just to let it be.

Chapter Twenty-Seven

I HAD A TECH conference to attend in Alexandria, Virginia, in early March. Rather than stay in a hotel, I thought I'd return the imposition and stay at Jackie's place. When I pulled up to her house in my tiny little rental vehicle, I felt like I was invited to a black-tie party, but I was wearing cut-off shorts. Her place was huge. Just short of a mansion. I had no idea she had been making the kind of money it would take to live here.

I arrived at dusk, and the decorative lighting on the outside of the house framed it in a gorgeous, warm setting. The grounds—and yes, when you have this much money, they can be called 'grounds' instead of just 'the yard'—were perfectly manicured. A hint of late winter snow on the ground gave it an idyllic look, like a house that would be featured in a movie about a wealthy family at Christmas.

I parked the car in the circular driveway and rang the doorbell. Jackie answered the door dressed in workout gear, holding a water bottle and sweating as if she had just come off the court.

"Hey! You made it. I hope it wasn't too hard to find."

"No, I had no problems finding it, probably because you can see this place from outer space. Geez, Jack. What the hell? When did you become filthy rich?"

"You're exaggerating. This is the smallest house in the area. And I told you my company was doing well when I saw you at Christmas."

"You didn't say you were doing this well. I'd have been more tempted to take you up on your offer to steal me away from Kelly if I'd known."

Jackie laughed as she hugged me and took my bag from me. "And if I'd known flashing my money around was all it took, I'd have done a better job of it. Come on in. The guest room is ready for you. How long are you staying?"

"The conference is three days, and there's a dinner on the last night, so I won't leave until the following day."

"What's the conference about?"

"It's a boring tech conference. I'm meeting one of my colleagues who works out of the D.C. office, and we're presenting our three-year roadmap. I may stay at her place the day after tomorrow since we'll be working together a lot, but I'm playing it by ear. Besides, I wanted to check up on you."

"Maybe I'm the one who needs to be checking on you. Does your wife know you're considering staying with a female colleague?"

"Of course she does. You know me, Jackie. I have no interest in anyone other than Kelly. She has nothing to worry about, and she knows it."

"Yeah, but what if this woman has different ideas? Have you considered that? It's kind of odd to invite a coworker to stay at your house, don't you think?"

"You're letting your imagination run wild," I said, as my phone started to ring. "Speak of the devil. Hey, Kel! Perfect timing. I just got here." She had FaceTimed me, so I turned the camera around so she could see Jackie. They were waving to each other when Kelly noticed my opulent surroundings.

"Where the heck are you guys?" she asked.

"This is Jackie's house if you can believe that! Holy shit, Kel. You should see this place. Jackie's been holding out on us. She's rich!"

"She's exaggerating, Kelly. I'm not rich. I'm 'comfortable.'" she said, making air quotes.

"Yeah, my parents always used to call people comfortable when they wanted to use a code word for rich. I'm impressed. Has my sister seen this place?"

"Yep. She's been here a couple of times already."

"Are you behaving yourself, Jackie?" Kelly asked.

"Yes, Kelly. We talk to each other every day. I haven't so much as looked at another woman since I left your house. You don't need to worry. Your sister has me all tied up in knots."

"Good. I hope it stays that way. I'm glad I sent Beth up there on this fake conference thingy so she could check up on you."

"It's not fake. It's..." I said, but Jackie quickly interrupted me.

"Hey, Kel. Did you know your wife has some woman colleague she's working closely with on this fake conference thingy?"

"Oh, you mean Emma? Yeah, I know. It's all good. I don't think Beth is the cheating type. Anymore." Ouch. That one hurt, but I let it go.

"I'll keep my eye on her, just in case. Turnabout is fair play, you know. If she's checking up on me, then I'm checking up on her."

"Excuse me, ladies," I chimed in. "I'm standing right here, you know. You don't have to talk about me as if I'm invisible. And there's nothing to check up on because Emma is a coworker, nothing more."

"We'll see," Jackie said and took off down the hall with my suitcase. "Talk to you soon, Kelly," she yelled as she left the room.

I pointed the camera back to me and looked closely at Kelly. She looked tired for some reason. Beautiful, but tired. "Hey, you're looking a little ragged. Are you alright?"

"Gee, thanks, babe. What a nice compliment."

"No, seriously. I just mean that you look really exhausted. Did you have a rough day today? It's just 'cause you miss me, right?"

"I'm fine. This case I'm working on is grueling, but the closing arguments are tomorrow, so it will all be over soon. For what it's worth, I do miss you, though."

"I miss you too. You know how much I hate going away without you. I feel like I'm missing a limb or something."

"Awww. That's sweet—kind of creepy—but sweet all the same. Okay, I'll let you get settled. I expect a full report tomorrow after you've had a chance to do some prying. I need to know if Jackie is treating my sister right."

"Don't you worry. I'll be sure to butt in where I don't belong. I love you, babe. Give my boys a pat on the head for me."

"Love you too!" The call disconnected, and Jackie came back into the room. She gave me a tour of the place, which was exquisitely decorated and furnished. Her kitchen was the size of the whole first floor of our house—marble countertops with top-of-the-line cooktop and ovens. The dining room table seated twelve, with a glistening chandelier over the table.

"Jackie, seriously. This house is…over the top. Are you the only one who lives here?"

"For now, yes." Jackie gave a cheeky grin as she led me to the guest room. "With any luck, I'll convince Paige to move in with me sooner rather than later."

"Really? Wow, you're moving fast. Are you sure about this?" I could see that my covert investigative work was starting before I even unpacked.

"Let's get you settled first. Meet me in the kitchen in a few minutes, and we can talk all about it."

Jackie departed, and I took a moment to unpack some of my things in the bathroom. I splashed some water on my face, then noticed as I was drying it that even the towels were expensive in this house. My king-sized bed had a pale printed duvet with matching shams on the pillows. I had no idea Jackie had a flare for decorating. Although, after further consideration, I decided that when you have this much money, you hire an interior designer. And this room just reeked of interior design.

I left my room and walked down the hallway, noticing there were dozens of pictures on the walls. Jackie's family was well represented, which was interesting since she wasn't particularly close to them. Her brother and his wife and kids looked adorable, and he hadn't changed a bit since I knew him all those years ago.

The rest of the pictures were obviously friends at places like P-Town and Fire Island. I even came across one of me and Kelly at a wedding we went to a year or two prior. I had no idea Jackie had become such a sentimentalist. I was pleasantly surprised to find several photos of Paige, both alone and together with Jackie. They had come a long way in the three months since we introduced them. They looked happy in these photos, and I was hoping that looks weren't deceiving.

Back in the kitchen-the-size-of-my-house, Jackie had poured us a couple glasses of wine. The back wall was floor-to-ceiling glass, and the view of the night skyline was stunning. I looked down to see a massive swimming pool below.

"Okay, before we discuss anything else, I have to ask. When the *hell* did you become this wealthy?"

"My business was acquired by another company a few years ago. They made me an offer I couldn't refuse."

"Why didn't you tell me?"

"What should I have done? Walked into your house and announced, 'Guess what? I just made an obscene amount of money! Besides, it's true what they say. It doesn't buy happiness."

"Paige must have been pretty shocked the first time she came here."

"She was. However, she's not the type to be impressed by money. Which, by the way, is an admirable quality, but that doesn't mean I won't shower her with gifts if she lets me."

"You're really serious about her, huh?"

"I think I want to marry her."

"What? You're kidding me."

"I wouldn't kid about a thing like that."

"Does she feel the same?"

"I think so. I hope so. We've seen each other almost every weekend since we left your house, and we FaceTime every day. I can't get enough of her."

"And you've kept your hands off all those women who seem to be drawn to you like moths to a flame?"

She made a cross-my-heart gesture and said, "Yep."

"Have you been tempted?"

"Not even once. I haven't gone out at all, so unless it's at work or the grocery store, I haven't even been in the presence of other women."

"I never thought I'd see the day," I said, with more than a hint of surprise in my voice. "My wife will be very relieved when I report back to her."

"She's coming down on Thursday, so you'll get to see her. Assuming you don't spend the night with your co-worker. Or should I say your lovah," she said with emphasis.

"I learned my lesson when you seduced me and made me cheat on Kelly all those years ago. Not going to happen again, believe me."

"I didn't *make* you do anything. As I recall, there were two willing participants in that hotel room. I didn't have to twist your arm."

"You plied me with alcohol and took me back to your room!"

"Face it, Beth. It may have been a mistake in judgment, but you and I always clicked in bed."

"That is true," I said reluctantly. "I hope the same can be said for you and Paige."

"You have no idea." Jackie smiled from ear to ear. "It's...euphoric. That's the only word I can come up with that even comes close to describing it."

"High praise, coming from you. You've pretty much done it all when it comes to sex. Any woman who can make you say euphoric has to be very special indeed."

"That's because, until now, I've never slept with a woman I'm in love with. Big difference."

"Don't I know it. It makes all the difference in the world. I'm happy for you, Jack. I just hope you still feel the way you do today when the shine wears off. Do me a favor, though, okay? Just wait a little while before you ask her to marry you. Maybe live together first. Once you start dealing with all the everyday bullshit of being together all the time, the real strength of the relationship becomes clear. It either works, or you realize it was just lust, not love."

"I'm going to ask her to move in when she comes this weekend. She'd have to quit her job, but she doesn't have to work if she doesn't want to. I'm happy to let her be a kept woman."

"Knowing her, she'll still want to work. She is a Gallagher, after all."

"I was thinking she could go back to school if she wants. She never got to have the career she wanted. Once she lost Lori, that was the end of that. It would make me really happy if I could help her get that back. Assuming she still wants it, that is."

"And what about you? Are you still working now that you've sold the company?"

"I'm still involved, but I've handed over most of my responsibilities. I'm trying to decide what I want to do next. I could start another company, but it would have to be in a different sector, based on the terms of the contract I signed for the sale. I might do some volunteer work. Maybe take Paige on an extended trip. Have a baby. I don't know."

I nearly spit out my wine. "Wait, wait, wait. Back up. What? Have a baby? Are you serious?"

"Totally serious. Being with Paige has made me want to do so many things I've never considered before."

"Whoa, whoa, Jackie. *Please* slow down. You're moving at lightning speed. These are all major life decisions, and you've only been together a few months."

"In the words of my favorite movie quote, 'when you realize you want to spend the rest of your life with somebody, you want the rest of your life to start as soon as possible.' That's from *When Harry Met Sally*, in case you were wondering."

"I know. It's my favorite movie too, remember? And while I can appreciate the sentiment, there are so many things that change after the relationship bliss wears off."

"Has yours worn off?"

"To some extent, yes. Once you're no longer having sex every day and finding every little habit 'adorable,'" I made a wildly exaggerated air quote gesture, "you have to make sure your love is strong enough to tolerate her and those habits when you discover they really *aren't* adorable and she annoys the crap out of you when you're trying to read, and she's whistling, or something like that."

"If that's the worst of it, I think we'll be fine."

"My point is that you don't know what those annoying little triggers are in only three months."

"I know you think I'm crazy. I get it. If the roles were reversed, I'd be giving you the same advice. And in fact, I think I did give you that advice."

"No, you just enticed me into bed in a misguided effort to prove that if I slept with you, Kelly must not be my one true love."

"Yeah, I did do that, didn't I?"

"So should I send a spy up to Brooklyn to sleep with Paige to do the same thing?"

"If you do, I will never speak to you again."

"Well, if I do and she turns the woman down, that would be a good sign, right?"

"Seriously. Do not do that."

"I'm kidding. Relax. Unlike you, I would never do that."

"That was the old me. The new me has changed my wicked ways."

"I really hope that's true, Jackie." I walked over to her and put my arms on her shoulders to make my point. "Don't screw this up. You've got a good thing."

"I know. I just hope I have the good sense to remember that whenever something tempts me."

"If you're tempted, think of it this way. You just described making love to Paige as euphoric. Is any one-night stand with a woman, regardless of how beautiful she may be, ever going to live up to that?"

"Nope. Not a chance."

"You've reached the point now where you have too much to lose. I realized that the day I left your hotel room and went to tell Kelly what had happened. I blew it. The best thing that had ever happened to me, and I blew it. I still can't believe she forgave me. Paige is not going to be as forgiving."

"I know. You're making me miss her even more than I already do. I wish she were here right now."

"You're funny; you know that?"

"What do you mean?"

"I'm just shocked and amazed at this transformation. And what's even funnier—not in a ha ha funny way, obviously, but an interesting way—is that you aren't even fighting this. You're just jumping right in. It's kind of sweet. I'm even a little jealous of you right now."

"What do you have to be jealous of? You have the perfect marriage."

"Nobody has a perfect marriage. That doesn't exist. But yes, I have a very good marriage. I'm lucky. I do miss that beginning part every once in a while, and I guess that's what I'm jealous of, but I wouldn't trade that for what we have now. Not a chance."

Chapter Twenty-Eight

WHEN I GOT BACK from the conference that Thursday afternoon, Paige met me at the door as I walked in. I gave her a big hug and couldn't help but notice how good she looked. That little hint of sadness in her smile was gone, and it did my heart a world of good to see it. *Wait 'til I tell Kelly*, I thought to myself. She'd act like she wasn't happy about it since it was Jackie that made it happen, but it would be just that—an act. Paige's well-being was more important than her need to be right. I loved that about her.

When Paige broke from our embrace, I noticed the absolutely stunning sapphire necklace she was wearing. It was small enough not to be ostentatious and yet big enough to be instantly drawn to it. She could see what I was looking at and commented.

"It's gorgeous, isn't it? She gave it to me last weekend. I cried. I've never owned anything this beautiful in my life."

"I guess you should start getting used to the finer things in life. I was shocked when I got here the other day. I knew Jackie was doing well, but I had no idea just how well. She said she wants to shower you with gifts."

"She knows I don't care about any of that stuff, but I let her give me this one because, well...I just couldn't resist it."

"Where is she anyway?" I asked, looking around the room.

"She's up in her office on a conference call. She'll be done in an hour or so."

I changed out of my suit and into jeans and a T-shirt, and we made our way out to the patio, it being a lovely pre-spring day. Paige had a pitcher of lemonade on the table and poured me a glass. Jackie's cat Snickers came out to greet us briefly, then did what cats do—he left us quickly and moved on to more interesting things. Paige told me about work and how she was trying to get her boss to give her more challenging assignments, but it was frustrating because he wasn't listening.

I couldn't help but recall my conversation with Jackie earlier in the week when she said Paige would need to quit her job in order to move down to D.C. Suddenly, that seemed like Jackie might have an easier time convincing her than anticipated.

"How are things in Brooklyn, besides work-related stuff?" I asked, fishing for information.

"Okay, I guess, but really, work is all I do there now since I've been here most weekends lately. Jackie came to my place once, but we didn't...well, um... we never left my bedroom." Her words indicated shyness in sharing that detail, but the expression on her face gave her away. Much like her sister, Paige has an unapologetically devilish side to her, and I recognized it coming through in her smile.

I held up my hand, shielding myself from additional details. "TMI, sister-in-law. I don't need to hear about your sex life."

"I would think you would be happy I finally have a decent sex life to discuss. It's been a while."

"I am. I just don't want to hear the details. You're like my little sister. I had enough conversations about that when you were staying with us. You should have seen your sister the morning after you stayed in the hotel with Jackie. She was imagining all sorts of depraved things Jackie was doing to you. It was *not* a pleasant morning. Even the dogs didn't want to be around her that day."

"Well, she wasn't wrong." Paige laughed as she said it, and I cringed just hearing about it. "Has Kelly gotten used to the idea yet? Whenever I talk to her, she seems fine, but I can't tell what she's hiding from me."

"She's fine. You know her. She's more bluster than anything else. She'd hand you the world on a silver platter if it were within her power. As long as you're truly happy, she'll be fine."

"Beth, I am *truly* happy. I mean, like, ecstatically happy. It should be a crime to feel this good."

"Jackie feels the same. I hope you know that. As soon as I got here, I could see that. It's written all over her face."

"I want to marry her, Beth." *Well, that's convenient*, I thought. But I felt the need to rain on Paige's parade just as I did for Jackie. I still thought they were moving too fast, even if they were on the same page with each other.

"Paige, I thi..."

"Don't say it! I know what you're going to say. We've both had this conversation with each other many times. It's fast. We know it, but I don't want to waste any more time, and neither does she."

"You aren't worried about her past?"

"No, I'm not. Are you?"

"Only a little. I worry that she's never dealt with some of the reasons she's been so promiscuous in the past, but I can tell that things are very different with you. Still, I would be remiss if I didn't caution you."

"Here's how I look at it. For almost twenty years, we've each been coping with the hands we were dealt in our own ways. I've kept mostly to myself with an occasional fling here or there. Jackie has done the opposite. She's found plenty of company along her way—fling or a one-night stand or what have you. We each adapted in ways that got us to this point, but neither method brought us joy.

"That's not to say we've been miserable all these years, but I think we can all agree that me keeping to myself and Jackie sleeping around isn't a long-term recipe for happiness for either of us. So now, we've stumbled upon something that has really turned the tables—for both of us. I don't want to keep to myself anymore. She says she doesn't want to sleep around anymore, and I believe her. So why shouldn't we jump in with both feet and enjoy a level of happiness that neither of us has been able to find on our own?"

"It's hard to argue when you put it like that."

Paige's phone blinged with the sound of a text message. She fished the phone out of her pocket to read it, and she smiled a great big toothy smile. "What?" I asked, smiling along with her.

"Nothing. Sexy text from Jack. Sorry."

"Oh geez. She sends you sexts when you're both in the same house at the same time?"

"Yep. I just told her you were home. She didn't know. She was summoning me to help her make her meeting more interesting."

"Ew," I said.

"You asked."

I sighed and got up from my chaise lounge by the pool. "Go have your fun," I said, and I gave her a dismissive but loving wave and made my way into my room. "Call me when y'all want to have dinner."

Chapter Twenty-Nine

AFTER BETH LEFT ON Saturday morning, Jackie and Paige took an afternoon drive to see the start of the cherry blossom blooms at the arboretum. With the top down on the BMW, they held hands and sang in harmony to every song on the Beatles' satellite radio station. At each red light, they leaned into each other and kissed.

Jackie smiled. "We're so corny, aren't we?"

"Yep. And I'm okay with that. You?"

"Yes. If only my twenty-year-old self could see me now. She'd be shocked and amazed."

They set up a blanket under a tree and watched the family on the blanket a few feet away feeding lunch to their little kids. The parents handed them their juice boxes and peanut butter and jelly sandwiches. A girl of about five wanted no part of the sandwich and was whining about the potato chips she just *knew* were buried at the bottom of mom's bag of goodies. Paige looked on with a smile, but Jackie's focus was elsewhere, watching Paige's reaction to the children.

"Do you want them?" Jackie asked.

"Want what? Peanut butter and potato chips? Yes, as a matter of fact."

"No, silly. Kids. Do you want kids?"

"I've thought about it, but it never seemed like a reality. I'm not getting any younger, so it seems even more unlikely now. How about you?"

"It never seemed likely for me either." Jackie paused and lowered her head, hesitant to express her next thought. "Until you…"

Paige choked on the water she was sipping. "Until me? What are you saying, Jackie? Do you want to have kids with me?"

"I've thought about it, but judging from your reaction, I'm guessing I'm way off base, huh?" Jackie stood up and paced around the picnic blanket.

"No, no. I didn't say that. You just caught me off guard. Way off guard. Being parents is…well, terrifying. And then there's the problem of finding the right donor. How do you pick some random person to be the dad? And how do you do that without knowing if, deep down, they have some deep-seated psychopathic tendencies?"

"I think that's a bit extreme, don't you? Maybe we should back up a bit. I didn't mean to scare you. I'm just thinking about the future, and that's a pretty big thing for me, you know? I usually don't plan more than a week or two ahead, except when it comes to my business."

"Spontaneity is not always a bad thing. It got us to where we are today, right?"

"That is true. If you didn't spontaneously ask me out, we probably wouldn't even be seeing each other right now."

"You weren't going to ask me out, were you?"

"Nope. I made a promise to your sister, and my plan was to keep that promise. *You* made me break it." Jackie crouched down to the blanket, her knees in front of Paige. She leaned in for a kiss, drawing a glare from the mother of the potato chip kid on the next blanket.

"Mmm…" Paige murmured and angled in for more. "We did more than break the promise that night. We shattered it. Crashed into a million shards of glass on the floor of the Marriott hotel where I threw myself at you."

"You were so sexy that night. In complete control. I loved every single second of it."

"You just weren't used to a woman calling the shots."

"You're right. I fell in love with you that night. I know exactly when it happened."

"What? When?"

"When you told me you were turning the tables on me to establish right off the bat that I am *not* the player in this relationship. Confidence is a very sexy quality, Paige. And you were so confident that night I had to restrain myself in the restaurant."

"We're not in a restaurant right now, so you don't have to restrain yourself."

"That woman over there begs to differ. She's giving us the evil eye." Jackie pointed to the blanket next to them.

"Too bad. Let her kids learn early that love comes in all different shapes and sizes." Paige pulled Jackie's face toward her and kissed her passionately. Jackie participated for a moment, then caught her breath and pulled away.

"I have an idea. Come on." She grabbed Paige's hand and lifted her off the ground. Jackie grabbed the blanket and their bag and guided Paige further into the wooded area, out of sight from all prying eyes.

Paige looked around, realizing they were secluded, and pushed Jackie against a tree before she could even get the blanket spread on the ground. "Are you gonna fuck me right here, babe?" she asked in a breathy, sexy voice.

"I hope so, but we have something to discuss first."

"Discuss? Now? Do you realize how horny I am?" Paige reached for Jackie's shirt, but Jackie pulled away.

"Paige...just give me five minutes of your attention, and then I promise, you can do with me what you will, okay?"

"Five minutes." She looked at her watch. "And not a minute more."

"Good. Now listen. I want to tell you something important." She spun Paige around so she was the one leaning up against the tree. "But first, you have to take that come hither look off your face because I can't concentrate."

"That's what you get for working me up."

"All I did was kiss you! You got worked up all on your own." They both laughed, and Paige tried hard to make a straight face while Jackie said what she needed to say.

"Maybe we should discuss this another time..." Jackie started to turn away, but Paige pulled her back and apologized.

"No, wait. I'm sorry, baby. Really. You obviously have something important you want to discuss, so please tell me what it is. You're actually making me a little nervous. Your body language is weird right now. Tell me what's going on."

"Okay. Listen. I've been thinking, and I want to ask you something. See, the thing is that these last three months have been the happiest of my entire life. I've put a lot of effort over the years into making sure I keep my distance from just about everybody in my life. A few weeks ago, you said that when I'm ready to tell you my deep dark secrets, you'll be here to listen to them. At the time, I thought, well, that probably won't happen because I won't give in and talk to you, and you won't stick around long enough to convince me that I should, but we're a little farther down the road now, and I think I was wrong.

"Yes, some things have happened to me that probably explains a lot about why I've done some stupid shit in my life. I want to share those things for the first time in my life. With you. And since I've never felt that way before, I've taken a good long look at what it is about you that's different."

Jackie let go of Paige's hands, took a deep breath, and reached into her pocket. She bent down on one knee and reached for Paige's hand again. Paige brought her other hand up to her mouth in shock.

"Paige, honey. I love you. I'm *in* love with you. I know it's soon, and Beth keeps telling me to slow down, but the truth is, I don't want to slow down. I want to start a life with you. Will you marry me, Paige? Please?" She held out a Tiffany ring box, open to a stunning princess-cut diamond.

Paige breathed heavily, taking the box from Jackie. Her hand trembled as she brought it closer, seeing its beauty. "Jackie. I'm... I'm speechless. I don't know what to say."

"Say yes. Say yes, and let me spend the next fifty years showing you what you mean to me, how you've changed my life, all for the better. Say yes so we can be a family."

"Jackie..." She threw her arms around Jackie's neck and whispered in her ear, "Yes. I love you so much. Yes. Yes..." She pulled away and looked at Jackie with those piercing blue eyes. "Yes!" she screamed. They locked in their embrace and cried together, kissing each other and wiping away their happy tears. Jackie turned around to see if anyone was around who might hear her.

"She said yes!" she screamed. "We're getting married!"

Peering from behind a tree in the distance, they could see the head of the woman whose family was sitting beside them earlier, looking at them judgmentally. "Don't worry, lady. We're keeping our distance from you! Your kids are safe!" Paige bellowed, and they laughed as they held each other. They noticed the woman was headed their way, and both stiffened in preparation for a homophobic encounter. "Uh-oh," Jackie said.

Jackie stood in front of Paige as she approached, instinctively shielding her from what might be coming their way.

"Hi, ladies." Paige noticed she had two cupcakes, one in each hand.

"Hello," Jackie said cautiously.

"I hope you don't mind. We couldn't help but overhear, and we wanted to say congratulations. My kids insisted I bring you these cupcakes to celebrate your wonderful news. May you have a long and happy marriage."

"Oh, wow," Jackie said. "I gotta be honest. I was expecting a much more negative response based on the look on your face when we were sitting over by you. I'm sorry I misjudged you."

"No apologies necessary. My husband always tells me I look mad when I'm not mad at all. In fact, he scolded me after you ladies moved your blanket. He said I chased you away. If I did, I'm very sorry. I didn't mean to do that. I'm happy to have my kids see *any* couple in love. No exceptions."

"Well, thank you for coming over. What's your name?"

"Liz." She reached out her hand to Jackie, then to Paige.

"Hi, Liz. My name is Jackie, and this is my fiancé, Paige. Wow, that's the first time I've ever used that word!"

"Feels pretty good, right? I remember after we got married. The first time I said husband, it kind of freaked me out." She gestured back toward her blanket. "Would you ladies like to come over and meet my family?"

"Thank you, Liz. It's very kind of you," Jackie said. "But, um...well...as you can imagine, I think we'd like to spend a little time alone and savor the moment."

"Sure, sure. Of course. I'm sorry for intruding on that. Congratulations again. Enjoy this time in your relationship! It's the best!"

"Thank you, Liz." As she walked away, Jackie put her arms around Paige again and spun her in celebration. She held her tight and started to cry again. "You've made me the happiest woman on the planet. Do you know that, Paige? I'm going to do everything I can to make sure I don't let you down."

"So, are you going to put this ring on my finger or what?"

"Oh, boy. I'm screwing up already. Liz got me all out of whack." She pulled the ring out of the box and took Paige's left hand, slipped the ring on, and admired it.

"It fits perfectly," Paige said, holding it up to look at it more closely.

"I measured one of your other rings when I was at your apartment a couple of weeks ago. I wanted to make sure I got it right." Paige put her hands on Jackie's face and pulled her in close, kissing her with more tears running down her cheeks. "I can't wait to make you my wife," she whispered in Paige's ear. She could feel Paige's heart beating through her chest, and she pushed back a bit to put her hand over Paige's heart. "Your heart is pounding."

"I know. I feel it. That's you. You're doing it to me." Paige's breathing continued to increase.

"Are you okay? You look like you might be hyperventilating. Sit down."

"I think I'm just overwhelmed with all kinds of emotions. I'm ecstatic, I'm excited, I'm horny, and I'm scared, all wrapped up in one. My breathing seems to be taking on a mind of its own."

"Why are you scared?"

"Jackie, the last time I let myself feel this way, it all came crashing down around me in the blink of an eye. Literally. It's scary to let my guard down again."

"I can understand that. And I can't promise you that nothing bad will ever happen to us. Neither can you. But maybe that will make us both appreciate each other even more."

They sat down on their blanket and wrapped themselves around each other. "So, there's another item we need to discuss," Jackie said.

"Uh-oh."

"When are you going to move in with me, Paige Gallagher?"

"Oh, wow. I didn't even think about that, but what about my job?"

"You can get another job anywhere. You're good at what you do. Or, you can choose not to work. You don't have to. You could even go back to school if you want."

"I'm way too old for that," Paige scoffed.

"Never too old. You have a million options at your disposal. Money is not a factor, so let your imagination run wild. What would you like to do?"

"Well, for one thing, I've never been supported by anyone before, so that might take a little getting used to. For now, I will need to pay my share."

"Paige, honey?"

"What?"

"Um…I'm not sure how to say this without sounding like a pompous asshole, but I…that is, we are…well, we're wealthy. And not just a little wealthy, but a lot. Like, money will never be an issue for us for as long as we live. If we have kids someday—and I'm not saying we will, but if we do—money will never be an issue for them for as long as they live. Okay?"

"Oh, wow. Um…I don't even know how to react to that information. I knew you had money, obviously. One just needs to look at your house to figure that out."

"Our house…"

"Not yet. You could still change your mind."

"No chance. We can go to my lawyer's office, and I'll put the deed in both our names right now if it will make you feel better."

"Jackie, I don't care about the house. I don't care about the money. It doesn't mean anything to me."

"It doesn't mean anything to me either. It's never made me happy, that's for damn sure, but some things are infinitely easier when you don't have to worry about money."

"Like what? Name one."

"Okay. I could have your entire apartment packed up, and everything moved, unpacked, and set up in our house in a matter of a day or two. You can't do things like that without money."

"Good point."

Jackie pulled her chin up to look Paige in the eye. "So, I propose that when we get back to the house this afternoon, you never leave, okay? How does that sound? I'll never have to say goodbye to you again. We'll make arrangements to get your stuff, you'll call your boss and tell him you quit, and we will live happily ever after."

Paige nuzzled Jackie behind the ear. "I do like the sound of that last part."

"So, what do you say?"

"I'd say yes to just about anything right now. I feel like I'm overdosing on dopamine. There's only one more thing that would put a cherry on top of this day."

"What's that?"

Paige kissed her softly at first but quickly intensified. She ran her hands through Jackie's hair, pulling her head back as she kissed her neck.

"You want to do this right here, baby?" Jackie asked.

Paige pushed her hands up under Jackie's shirt. "Right here, right now."

"Babe, there are people around."

"I don't care. Let them find their own partners to fuck in the park."

Paige pushed Jackie onto her back and straddled her with her knees at the waist. She pulled her shirt and bra over her head, and grabbed for Jackie's hands to reach up and touched her breasts. Her pelvis was grinding into Jackie's, begging for attention. She leaned in and put her nipples in Jackie's mouth while she reached in between their stomachs to undo Jackie's Levi's. She rolled them both into the excess of the blanket, giving them a sliver of privacy. She eased down to yank Jackie's pants off of each leg. Jackie panted with anticipation, no longer caring they could probably be seen by anyone who may walk by. The need to be satisfied by Paige far overshadowed any fear of discovery.

Paige entered her, pushing in and pulling out at a furious pace. Jackie tried to contain her screams, but she eventually gave in to them as Paige pulled her fingers away and replaced them with her tongue, darting up and down, in and out. As Jackie was about to come, Paige stopped and looked up at her, both gasping for breath.

"Why are you stopping?" Jackie screamed.

"Because I want you to say it."

"Wha..." Jackie panted. "Say what?"

"Tell me how you want me to finish you off."

"Paige, please." Jackie grabbed her head and pushed it between her legs. "Please..." Paige did as she was told and dove back in until she made her scream. Then she wrapped them tightly in the blanket like a burrito and held Jackie through her aftershocks, whispering in her ear as she trembled. She could hear Jackie crying softly.

"Shhh...it's okay, baby. I've got you. Let it all go. I've got you." She kissed Jackie's tears and brushed the hair off her face. They looked at each other and smiled.

Jackie considered their situation, being naked and somewhat exposed in a public park. She laughed and said, "Something tells me that being married to you is going to be one hell of an adventure."

Chapter Thirty

WHEN I GOT HOME FROM D.C. on Saturday afternoon, my wife peppered me with questions about the state of the Paige/Jackie union. She seemed relieved that things were going well, but in typical Kelly fashion, she hesitated to be optimistic. I was careful in my wording of their current status, avoiding the admission by both parties that they wanted to get married. Kelly didn't need to know that just yet. No need to cause angst until, or unless angst was warranted. Especially since I'm the one who would have to listen to the angst-laden complaining.

In the meantime, when I returned, I couldn't help but notice Kelly was looking especially run down. As I stared at her across the kitchen, I could see the bags under her eyes. Kelly's never had bags under her eyes, regardless of how hard she worked. Her skin is flawless, taut as a trampoline.

I knew this case she was working on was tough, but all her cases were tough. It came with the territory of being a lead prosecutor. I watched her throughout the evening and started to worry something was wrong. She was in and out of the courtrooms, dealing with all kinds of people. I was afraid she might have Covid.

"Hey, honey," I started, treading lightly.

"Yeah?"

"Are you feeling alright?"

"Sure. Why?"

She didn't sound very convincing. "Well, you just look a little rough around the edges."

"You said that on the phone the other day. It's not exactly a compliment. What are you trying to say, babe?"

"I'm a little worried, that's all. You look exhausted. Have you tested yourself for Covid lately?"

"We have to test once a week, so yes. I am negative. I'm just tired."

"Maybe you need a day off. Or a week off. Or maybe you need to see a doctor."

Kelly hesitated, went to the coffee pot to refill her cup, then looked back at me. "I've been to the doctor."

"What? Why didn't you tell me? Since when do we see doctors without telling each other?"

"You were away, and I didn't want to worry you."

"I know you, Kelly. There's no way you would see a doctor unless there was something else besides just being tired. What the hell is going on?" My voice was raised because I was really pissed off that she hadn't said anything to me.

"Okay, okay. Please don't be upset with me." She came over and grabbed my hands, trying to de-escalate. "I've had a few dizzy spells. And I fainted on my way into the courtroom the other day. It's no big deal. I went to see my regular doctor yesterday, and she sent me for a CT scan. We should have the results on Monday. I'm sure it's nothing to worry about."

"So, wait a second. Let me get this straight. You saw the doc yesterday, and she sent you for a CT scan the very same day? And you're telling me not to worry?"

"The place is right there on-site with the doctor's office. I'm sure they do that all the time," she said, sounding like she was trying to convince herself as much as me. It wasn't working for either of us.

"Do you have a follow-up appointment?"

"No. She wanted to look at the scan first and then call me." I started pacing the room without realizing it, so she grabbed my arm to get me to stand still. "Can we please not panic about this?"

I pulled away and resumed my pacing. "What else have you kept from me so that you 'wouldn't worry me?'" I said, with unnecessarily exaggerated air quotes. I was mad at her, and I was mad at myself for being mad at her. She should have told me when she fainted. The fact that I was away for a few days shouldn't have had any bearing on the situation.

"I've been getting some headaches," she said meekly.

I was on the verge of another angry reaction when something made me pause for a second and look over at her. She was scared, and I was making it worse. I took a deep breath and went over to her, putting my arms around her waist. "How long have you had the headaches?"

"A few months. They started around the time Paige and Jackie were here, so I chalked them up to stress."

"Okay. I'm sorry I got mad. I just...we're not supposed to keep secrets like that, Kel. If one of us is sick, the other needs to know about it. What if the tables were turned, and I didn't feel well, went to the doctor, and had a scan all without telling you?"

"I'd be furious."

"Well, at least we agree on that. How are you feeling today? Do you have a headache?"

"Yes. It's not too bad, though. Just dull but persistent."

"Okay, let's get you into bed then."

"Babe, I don't need to go to bed. I just have a headache. Please don't make this out to be more than it is."

"Okay," I said reluctantly. "I'll try, but this is going to be a really long weekend."

"Take my mind off this, please. Tell me something about your trip."

"Well, the work stuff was boring, but my presentation with Emma went well. Jackie was all up in my case about working so closely with her. She wanted to make sure I wasn't cheating on you."

"Yeah, I'm not worried about that."

"Why? You don't think I could get Emma in bed?"

"I'm sure you could, but you won't."

"You're right, and I won't." She knew me too well. "Okay, so the rest of the trip was interesting. First, let me say I had no idea Jackie was so rich. That house is over the top. Every detail is top of the line. I can't even imagine what it cost. Your sister is going to make out pretty well in that department. She was sporting a lovely sapphire necklace when I saw her."

"Oh, so you think they're going to stay together?"

"Well, I'm not going to answer that until I know whether the answer will make you happy or mad."

"I've decided just to let it play out however it's supposed to play out. I've expressed my concerns, and now I have to let them be adults and figure it all out. My sister is tough. She's not going to take any shit from Jackie, so if there is shit happening, the relationship will end."

"That's an excellent way of looking at it."

"And now that you know I won't be mad...what's the answer to my question?"

"They both told me they want to get married." I cringed and waited for the reaction. She just sighed.

"Okay then. I really hope it works out for them. I mean that. I will happily say I'm sorry to both of them if Jackie proves me wrong."

"If my opinion counts for anything, I think they'll be okay."

"Let's just hope you're right. I'm tired of worrying about it, to be honest. We have other things to focus on."

"You mean like this test result."

"Yep."

* * * *

We went to bed unusually early that night. I could tell her headache was bothering her, and the stress of it was wearing her out. We turned on the television and held each other while we watched *Fried Green Tomatoes* for about the fiftieth time. I love that movie, mostly because I had a massive crush on Mary Stuart Masterson. She is super sexy in that role.

But as we got near the end, it occurred to me that maybe Kelly picked this on purpose and not in a good way. The heartbreaking ending was not one I wanted to see while we were waiting to hear CT scan results. I tried to get her to turn it off by fooling around with her, but she wasn't in the mood. So I just told her I was bored with it, and we moved on to something stupid on Netflix. About halfway through that show, the phone rang. It was a FaceTime call from Paige and Jackie.

"Are you two in bed at six in the evening on a Saturday? Geez, you never stop, do you?" Paige asked, before we even said hello.

"As a matter of fact, we are," Kelly answered, letting Paige's assumption linger in the air as if it was the truth rather than telling her she didn't feel well. I saw Jackie lurking in the background while Paige and Kelly caught up on mundane stuff, but then she came into the frame, and Paige brought her left hand up to the camera. "Oh my god!" Kelly said with at least some level of enthusiasm.

"We're engaged! Jackie asked me today when we were at the park. Isn't it gorgeous?"

I decided to fill in some of the blank space, giving Kelly a chance to decide on her reaction. "It's beautiful, Paige. Nice job, Jackie. I see you took my advice and slowed things down a bit."

"Yeah, well. I heard your advice loud and clear. And then I decided to ignore it. I couldn't wait any longer. I want to be Paige's wife."

"We're going to have my stuff moved here. I'm not going back to New York. I'm here for good now."

"I'm really happy for both of you."

"So am I," Kelly said, much to my surprise. "I know I've given you two a pretty hard time about this, but now that you've decided to give this a shot, I wish for a long and very happy marriage."

Paige smiled and put her hand on her heart, indicating she was touched by Kelly's words. "Thanks, Kel. That means a whole lot to me. I was worried about how you were going to react."

"I'm going to take good care of her, Kelly. I promise," Jackie said.

"You'd better," Kelly said. "When's the wedding?" Kelly and I both asked in unison.

"We're not sure yet, but soon. I want to make it legal, so Paige has access to everything around here," she motioned her arms around the house. "I've already talked to my lawyer, and we're modifying the deed to the house."

Paige barely let her finish that thought before she chimed in. "I tried to tell her she needs a prenup, but she's ignoring me. Kelly, as a lawyer, can you please advise her that she *needs* a prenup?"

"No!" Jackie said forcefully. "No prenup. End of discussion. We share everything from this point forward. I won't have it any other way. Okay?"

"Jackie..." Kelly tried to interject, unsuccessfully.

"End of discussion. I won't budge on this point," she insisted. "So, Beth, I have a question for you."

"Go for it," I said.

"Will you be my best woman? After all, this wouldn't have happened without you. I can't think of anyone else I'd want to stand up with me."

"I'd be honored, Jackie. I'll be sure to get you to the church on time."

"It probably won't be a church, but your point is still taken. Thanks, my friend. And Kelly, I'm feeling pretty lucky that I get to have you as my sister-in-law. I know we haven't always seen eye to eye, but I have mad respect for you, and I'm not going to let you down."

"Thanks, Jack. I see getting engaged has brought out your sentimental side."

"Yeah, well...finding the love of your life will do that." She gave Paige a smooch on the cheek.

"Kelly, will you help me with some of the planning?" Paige asked. "I really want your opinions. I don't even know where to start."

"Of course, sweetie. Just let me know when you want to talk about it."

"Okay. I love you guys. Have a good night!"

When the call disconnected, Kelly took her place in the crook of my arm again, and I could tell she was tired.

"Let's go to sleep, honey. We can talk about whatever you're feeling about this in the morning." I kissed her forehead, and she was asleep in a matter of minutes.

Chapter Thirty-One

WHEN MONDAY FINALLY ROLLED around, Kelly took the day off from work because her head was really bothering her. I refused to leave her alone, so I also took the day off. In hindsight, perhaps I should have gone to work, because we both spent the day looking at our respective watches and waiting for the phone to ring. I was probably making Kelly more anxious with my presence.

At about 1:00 PM, her doctor finally called. Kelly put her on speaker so we both could hear the results, but instead of giving us any information, she told us she needed to see us in person.

"Doctor, is that really necessary? Surely you can save me a trip and tell me what you've found over the phone."

"Kelly, I think you should come in so we can talk."

"When?"

"I'm here until five. I think you should come in right away if you can."

"You're freaking me out, Doctor."

"I know, Kelly, and I'm sorry about that. We'll discuss it when you get here."

She disconnected the call, and I noticed Kelly had gone completely pale. I'm sure if I had a mirror, I would have found the same to be true for my face. I could think of no possible good outcome when the doctor says you must come in immediately to discuss your test results, but for Kelly's sake, I had to find some strength to maintain my composure.

"Okay. So, let's get going. We aren't going to be able to relax until we know what she has to say, so we might as well go now." I started getting ready, putting on my shoes, and picking up my keys. I noticed Kelly was frozen in her chair. Without saying anything, I went to her and lifted her arm, encouraging her to get the rest of her body to follow. It took a few tries, but she finally complied, and I helped her to the bench by the front door, where she kept her shoes.

As I was tying her shoes, she said, "Beth, I have a horrible feeling about this."

"I know. Whatever it is, we'll deal with it, okay? One step at a time."

* * * *

As soon as we got to the office and gave the receptionist Kelly's name, she led us back to the doctor's office and not into an exam room. This made me even more anxious if that was possible. The office was not at all like what you see on TV shows. It was small and sparsely decorated, as if she didn't really spend much time there, so didn't bother decorating it.

There were typical diplomas on the wall, and I felt comforted that Dr. Wilson had graduated from Emory University, a top-notch school. A box of Kleenex sat strategically placed closest to the patient's side of the desk. I sent up a prayer to the universe that we would *not* need those tissues. I assumed the chairs we were sitting in were slightly upgraded so we could feel comfortable while we were getting bad news.

Dr. Wilson arrived with what I assumed was Kelly's patient file folder in her hands. It was relatively thin, indicating Kelly's good health thus far. We hadn't needed to be here all that often, thank goodness.

"Hi, ladies. Nice to see you again. Kelly, I'm glad you brought Beth with you. We need to talk about your test results." She logged into her computer and pulled up Kelly's scan. I guess the days when they put a film up on a lighted box on the wall were long gone. It's all digital now. She turned her computer monitor toward us so we both could see the result. Then, with the top of her pen, she pointed to the area of the scan that concerned her.

"You can see a mass here, at the base of the brain. It's about the size of a kiwi at this point, but I suspect it's been there for a little while, and it's growing. This would explain why you're suddenly having more headaches and dizziness. We need to get this removed as soon as possible."

"You mean brain surgery?" Kelly asked incredulously.

"Unfortunately so. I know that phrase strikes fear in your hearts, but there is still the possibility that it's not cancerous. We won't know until we get it out and test it. The good news is that it's positioned such that I think we can get to it pretty easily to remove it. You'll have an incision at the base of your skull, probably about an inch long."

I grabbed Kelly's hand because I could see out of the corner of my eye that she was about to lose it. "When do we need to do this?" she asked.

"Soon. Immediately, actually. I'd like to admit you tonight, and I've arranged with the neurosurgeon to get you into the OR first thing in the morning. Her name is Dr. Swanson, and she's one of the very best in Atlanta."

I could feel my heart rate increasing, and I took some deep breaths to quell the urge to hyperventilate. *This can't be real,* I thought. *This only happens in movies.* I stared at that kiwi on the computer screen. I realized my mouth was hanging open, and I quickly corrected that, maintaining what little composure I had for Kelly's sake.

"Okay. So, what do we do now?" I asked.

"Go home, pack a few things in a bag, and head right over to Emory. I'll have your admission paperwork waiting there for you. They'll get you settled. Don't eat or drink anything after six tonight. We'll have you in the OR by about seven in the morning."

"What are the chances I won't make it through this surgery, Doctor?" Kelly asked.

"You're young and healthy. All surgery has inherent risks, but I'm confident the procedure itself will be fine. Obviously, I can't predict what happens next until we get it out and tested. Kelly, Beth, I know I've given you quite a shock today, and believe me, it's not something I take lightly. You will get the very best care. I've known Dr. Swanson for a long time, and I would trust her with my own life. Let's take this one step at a time. We'll get it out, then see what happens next."

We left Dr. Wilson's office in a semi-catatonic state. I held Kelly's hand and led her to the car. I'm not really sure how I got us home because I don't remember driving at all. All I could hear were the words brain surgery.

I got Kelly into the house and sat her down on the couch while I went to put some of her things in a bag. I decided to pack a bag for myself as well because I had no intention of leaving that hospital until Kelly was seated in the passenger's seat of the car, ready to go home.

I called our neighbor and asked if they could watch the dogs for us for a few days. I was going to call Paige, but decided to wait until I got her settled in her room. I wanted to talk to Paige when Kelly was out of earshot, so now was not the time.

True to her word, Dr. Wilson had made all the arrangements, and we made it through the admission process pretty quickly. When they sent us to the person who collects our insurance info, I tried not to panic when I heard her say this procedure could run up into the six-figure range, and she couldn't say for sure how much our insurance would cover. So on top of the stress of brain surgery, I needed to worry about going bankrupt in the process. Expressing concern at that moment seemed to be a waste of energy since the woman taking our information obviously had no control over it at all.

Once they took us upstairs, they put us in a private room, thankfully. The nurse came in to get her set up with an IV for fluids. I tried to engage in light banter to help ease Kelly's nerves, but I knew there was nothing I could say that was going to take away her fear. I knew this because there was nothing anyone could say to *me* at this point to take away my fear. A vision of my life without Kelly flashed before my eyes. It was a dark and dismal thought, and I couldn't believe this was suddenly our lot. Until a few hours ago, our biggest concern was whether or not Jackie would break Paige's heart. And now we were in a life-and-death situation.

Speaking of Paige, I waited until Kelly was hooked up to her IV and settled in her bed before heading out into the common area to make a few phone calls. Paige was high on the list, but I had to make sure both Kelly's boss and mine knew we would be out for an unknown period of time. We're both so lucky to work for good people, and they responded to my news by saying we should take as much time as we need to get Kelly well. At least that was one less thing to worry about.

I had to think for a minute before I called Paige because the approach was crucial. I needed to let her know it was critical without getting her too worried or upset. That seemed impossible, but I tried anyway.

"You're where? For what?" she said when I told her we were at Emory because Kelly needed surgery. "What kind of surgery?"

"Brain," I said, then waited for the onslaught of questions and tears. When she went silent, I gave her a little more detail. "There's a mass of some kind near the brain's stem. They need to get it out as soon as possible and do a biopsy." Without realizing I'd lost her, I suddenly found myself talking to Jackie instead of Paige. I filled her in on what little we knew at this point.

"We're on our way," Jackie said. "We'll be there in a few hours."

"Jackie, I don't think that's necess…"

"We're on our way." She hung up.

I called Kelly's mom in Tucson and gave her the same news. She was not in good health herself, suffering some complications from diabetes, so she was not in a position to hop on a plane like Paige and Jackie. I promised to keep her posted every step of the way, and I talked her through her tears before I hung up with her.

When I returned to the room, a neurosurgery resident was taking Kelly's medical history and giving her information about the surgery before having Kelly sign the consent form.

"Do you have an advanced directive or a DNR on file?" he asked.

"No. I'm thirty-five years old and in good health. Why would I need that?"

"We have to ask. Surgery comes with risks, and brain surgery has the possibility of even more complications. We need to know your wishes in the event something goes wrong."

"My wishes are that you do everything humanly possible to save my life."

"Do you wish to be kept on life support?"

"That depends on the chances of recovery."

"Do you want to designate someone as your health care proxy, to make decisions as to your care if you are unable to do so?"

"Yes. My wife. You're sitting right next to her."

"Hello," I said quietly. "I'm Beth Farley."

"It's nice to meet you, Mrs. Farley. I will prepare some papers that both of you need to sign. I'll be back in a little while."

He left the room, and Kelly burst into tears. I sat down next to her, and we cried together. I didn't even attempt the hollow words I knew wouldn't register with her in this state of mind. I just held her and told her I was there no matter what.

After all the forms were signed and the comings and goings of the hospital staff finally stopped for the night, I crawled in bed beside her, and we whispered in the dark.

"We need to talk about what happens if this doesn't go well," she said, kissing my cheek.

"No, we don't. I don't want to. It's going to be fine. In about twelve hours, you'll be back here in the room all drugged and groggy, and we'll be talking about what you want for lunch. I can't have this conversation with you, baby."

"Beth, listen. I need to say this, just in case. Please?"

"Okay," I said reluctantly.

"If I'm a vegetable, I need you to talk to all the doctors. Get as many opinions as you need. If there's no chance I will recover, you have to let me go. I don't want to live on life support forever. But if there is a sliver of hope, I'll be fighting for us. Understood?" I did not react.

"And if you have to let me go, I want you to get on with your life. Do *not* do what my sister did and close yourself off for over a decade. You're too young for that. You're allowed to mourn me for a little while, and then you have to go back to living. Find someone to love, someone to spend the next chapter of your life with.

Understood?" She saw me crying and kissed me, her tears flowing freely.

"I'm not sure I would know how to do that, but I've heard your wishes," I said, sobbing by this point.

"Just try for me. You've been the best wife, Beth. I couldn't ask for more. I've been so lucky to have you. If I die, know that when we were together, I was truly happy. Okay? And tell Jake and Ollie they are the best boys, and I love them."

"You are not making this easy, Kel," I said through my tears. She kissed my cheeks again, wiped them with her thumb, and then kissed my lips softly. "Our story is not over," I said. "It can't be. You're going to come through this, and we will have decades before we leave each other. I refuse to say goodbye to you tonight. Is that understood?"

She nodded. I sniffled, then leaned over to the rolling bedside table and grabbed a tissue for each of us. We blew in unison, and we laughed. As we settled back in, the door opened, and Paige and Jackie walked in.

"Oh, geez. I must be dying. You've called in my sister."

"Very funny," Paige said. "But dying is strictly prohibited, so figure out another way to deal with this, please." She came over to the bed and fell into Kelly's arms. I got up and let them have their moment. Jackie came over to hug me and whispered in my ear.

"Paige is distraught."

"I'm sure she is, but we all need to just get through these next twenty-four hours before we know whether we even have something to be distraught about. How the hell did you get here so fast? We only spoke a few hours ago."

"I hired a private jet."

"Perks of being rich, huh?"

"Yeah, but too bad it can't buy health. If I could throw money at this problem to make Kelly well, I hope you know I would in a heartbeat."

"Thanks. I know that. And we may need to take you up on that when this operation runs into the six-figure range and depletes every savings account and credit card we have. How do poor people pay a bill like that?"

"They don't. They die. But luckily, you don't need to worry about that. I will take care of this."

"That's not what I meant, Jackie…"

"Beth, shut up. I've got it, okay? One less thing to worry about."

We both watched Paige and Kelly talking, a mixture of laughter and tears that broke my heart.

"So, what happens now?" Jackie asked.

"The surgeon will come to talk to us first, and then they'll take her down at about six tomorrow morning."

"Are you confident in this surgeon? Because we can get the best of the best here from anywhere in the world."

"We haven't met her yet, but we're told she's one of the best in Atlanta."

Jackie pulled out her phone and started Googling. "What's her name?"

"Swanson. First name is Michelle, I believe. Emory Neurosurgery." Jackie started researching her background, education, and reputation. Then she stepped out of the room to make a call. Paige had nuzzled herself in the crook of Kelly's arm, and I thought about how even when Kelly was the one in crisis, she was comforting Paige. It was so typical of their relationship.

When Jackie returned, she took me aside to tell me what she had learned. "So, I made a couple of calls to some hospital bigwigs I know. They've heard of Dr. Swanson and feel confident she's an excellent surgeon, but it's not too late to call in the best in the world if you want to go that route."

"No. Let's meet Dr. Swanson and take it from there. Unless something about her makes me nervous, I think we should proceed with her."

"Okay. So now let's talk about you. How are you holding up?"

"I'm numb. We've had conversations about DNRs and advanced directives. Yesterday we were talking about going to the movies this weekend. How did we get from there to here?"

Jackie put her arms around me and I held on tight, searching for any scrap of comfort or strength I could find. "We signed a health care proxy, meaning I have to decide what to do if something goes wrong, but how? How am I supposed to make that decision? She's my whole life."

"It's not going to come to that, Beth. And even if the worst possible thing happens, you won't have to do any of this alone."

* * * *

Jackie and I took turns 'sleeping' in the chair in Kelly's room and the chairs out in the hallway. I left Paige in the bed with Kelly, and they managed to get a few hours of sleep, but I was awake all night. Jackie poked her head back into the room at about 5:00 AM and motioned for me to come out into the hall. She had three cups of coffee in one of those cardboard cup-carrier things, and I happily took one from her.

"I didn't want to bring coffee into the room since Kelly can't have any. That would be cruel punishment."

"I know she would appreciate that. Thank you."

"You look like hell, by the way."

"Gee, thanks."

"No problem." She smiled at me and put her arm on my shoulder in reassurance. We noticed a woman in scrubs headed our way from down the hall, and I tensed, sensing it was probably the surgeon. *Here we go*, I thought to myself.

"Good morning. Is one of you ladies Beth Farley, by chance?"

"Yes, ma'am. That's me."

"I'm Dr. Swanson. I'll be doing the surgery on Kelly today. Is she still asleep?"

"Yes. Her sister Paige is with her, and this is Paige's fiancé, Jackie." They shook hands.

"Nice to meet you both. Shall we go in and wake your wife? Then we can talk about the procedure and I can answer your questions." She noticed I was crying and looked at me with genuine concern. "Beth. Is it okay if I call you Beth?" I nodded. "I know you're scared. I will do everything in my power to ensure Kelly is back in this room and talking to you in a few hours, okay?" I nodded, and Jackie put her arm around me as we entered the room.

Dr. Swanson spent about thirty minutes with us, explaining the procedure and what we should expect. She said they would not know the extent of the situation until they got in there. She had seen similar tumors that literally fell out as soon as she opened the skull, and she'd seen others that required a more intricate removal process. The tumor would be sent off for a biopsy, and we would have the results in about forty-eight hours or less. She said the chances that it was malignant were probably about 50/50. The surgery could be as short as two hours or as long as five or six. Kelly would probably be in the hospital for two or three days, depending on what they found.

We decided not to discuss the next steps for treatments just yet. "Let's get through the surgery first and then take it from there, okay?" I found her very reassuring, and by the look on Kelly's face, I think she did as well. "The nurse will be in to shave your hair in a few minutes." Kelly groaned, making it very clear she did not like this news. In typical Paige style, she chimed in and said, "You're having brain surgery, for fuck's sake. What did you expect?"

After the hair was cut and her scalp was shaved, Jackie and Paige left the room to give Kelly and me a chance to be alone before they took her down. I sat beside her, bringing her hand to my face. "Okay, my love. You have one job today. To meet me back here in a few hours. Failing at this job is not an option. Is that understood?"

"Yes, dear," she said, placating me. "But remember what you promised me yesterday if it all goes south."

"We're not discussing that today. We're only putting positive thoughts out into the universe."

"Okay, okay. But remember this. You are the love of my life. My days have been infinitely better because you were there. Never forget that, alright?"

I leaned into her, and we cried together. "I love you, Kel. Words fail right now. You be strong for me, and I'll be strong for you. I'll see you as soon as they let me see you. Do you want to talk to Paige again before you go?"

"No. We said it all last night. I'm ready to go." I went to the door and told the orderly that he could take her away. As he got her into the hallway, I saw Jackie stop them, and she leaned in, whispering something to Kelly. Kelly smiled, and they rolled her away.

Chapter Thirty-Two

AFTER THREE AND A half hours, my anxiety took over, and I could no longer contain my agitation. I paced around the waiting area in a trance-like state. Both Jackie and Paige tried unsuccessfully to console me. I had a bottle of water in my hands as I walked in circles, and when I accidentally bumped into a chair, I threw the bottle across the room in exploding frustration. Thankfully I didn't hit anyone. The wall took the brunt of the punishment, and since it was only water, no damage was done. As Jackie cleaned up the mess, Paige came over and sat me down.

"I' m not going to try to talk you down from this ledge, Beth. That would be a futile task. But I am going to try to keep additional objects from flying across the room. I'm sure we can find another, less destructive way to release some tension. Want to hear my suggestions?"

"I know, I know. I'll contain myself."

"We're in a hospital, so I'm sure I can find a pillow for you to scream into. Want one?"

"No, I'm okay now. I'll be a good girl. I just thought they would be done by now, and I keep thinking the longer it takes, the worse the news." I put my head into my hands. "What if it's bad news, Paige? What do we do then? How do we handle that?"

"I know it sounds trite to say, but the only answer I can give you is one day at a time."

"What if I'm not strong enough for her?"

"Oh, please. I've seen you handle her when she doesn't even know she's being handled. You know how to take care of her better than anyone. And you have me to pick up the slack when you need it. *If* you need it, but you're jumping the gun. We don't even know what we're dealing with yet." As Paige finished her sentence, the double doors outside the waiting room opened, and Dr. Swanson approached us.

"The surgery went well, and she's in recovery." We all gasped with relief. "Brain surgery always requires very heavy sedation, so she's not going to be conscious for a while, but as soon as she comes around, I'll let you see her for a few minutes. As for the tumor, it required a bit of finesse to remove, which is why it took as long as it did. It was attached to a thick section of blood vessels, and we had to be meticulous about it. But it's out, and I'm confident we got it all. Now we wait for the results."

My tears started flowing again, but these were happy tears. Happy she made it through the surgery and happy that, for now at least, I could breathe, knowing she was still breathing. Paige hugged me, and Jackie reached her arms around both of us. It felt like a victory, even if it could eventually be short-lived.

* * * *

An hour later, they let me into recovery to see her. The bandages on her head were frightening, and she was still hooked up to tubes and gadgets. She didn't look conscious, so I approached cautiously, putting my hand on her hand.

"I'm here, baby. You're okay." She moved her hand in mine. I could see she was trying to open her eyes and make a sound, but so far, neither had happened. So I sat and talked to her. I told her how I defaced public property by throwing my water bottle against the wall. Then I blamed it all on her. "Your sister and future sister-in-law are in the lobby waiting to see you." That seemed to get her attention, and she grunted at me.

"I knew that would wake you up." I smiled at her. "You don't have to talk if you don't feel ready yet. The Doc says they got the tumor out and everything went as expected. Now we wait for the results, which will happen in a day or so. All you need to do right now is rest. They said you'd be back in your room in about two hours. They aren't going to let me stay, and I promised Paige she could have a minute with you. So, get some sleep, baby. You did your job today."

I leaned in to kiss her forehead, and she opened her eyes. She couldn't quite form words yet, but she smiled at me and tightened her grip on my hand. I smiled back and left the room. I sent Paige into the room, and I went to the restroom. Then I locked myself in a stall and cried my eyes out.

* * * *

They brought her back to the room a couple of hours later. She was still very groggy, but she was able to speak softly. Hearing her form words gave me a great sense of relief. The doctor said she didn't expect speech or brain functions to be impacted, but I wasn't going to believe it until I heard it for myself. Then she asked for food, which was another good sign. The nurses came and went every few minutes, taking blood, checking vitals, and generally disrupting Kelly's sleep. They were afraid she would be nauseous, so she had to settle for some lime Jell-O and dry toast. Better than nothing, I suppose, but barely.

I kept a keen eye on her as she slept, watching for signs of trouble. The machines beeped at a constant pace, and the numbers on the screen didn't vary much from beep to beep. I had this thought that I knew was irrational, but it kept coming to me anyway. This giant green kiwi-shaped monster that loomed over the room yesterday was gone. The air felt different. Cleaner. Less invasive.

I imagined the blood flow in her head, running smoothly now without having to traverse the roundabout at the base of her brain. Whether the monster left behind its damaging debris remained to be seen, but at least it was gone.

Paige and Jackie went to our house to check on the dogs and pick up a few things. I took advantage of the time alone with Kelly sleeping, reflecting on all that had happened and all that was to come. Sorrow and joy were in the room with Kelly and me at that moment, like Schrödinger's cat. She's sick, and she's well at the same time. We wouldn't know which until we opened the box.

Chapter Thirty-Three

BY WEDNESDAY AFTERNOON, KELLY was getting anxious and restless. She wanted her results, and she wanted out of the hospital. Nothing else would make her happy until those two items could be checked off her list. Since it hadn't been forty-eight hours yet, I didn't feel like I could go complaining to the doctor, but she was really starting to get cranky with everyone she came in contact with, so I caved and called Dr. Swanson's office. The receptionist told me the doctor was at the hospital now doing rounds, so we could expect to see her before the end of the day.

As I delivered the news to Kelly, Paige, and Jackie, the doctor appeared as if by magic. I went to Kelly's side and instinctively grabbed her hand. I could feel my heart pounding and adrenaline sending an uncomfortable surge through my body. If Kelly was feeling the same, she was hiding it well because she smiled at Dr. Swanson and exchanged pleasantries I was incapable of.

The doctor had an iPad in her hand, tapping away at it to retrieve Kelly's files. She asked Kelly how she was feeling, whether the pain at the incision site was hard to handle and if she'd had any headaches. If I were answering, I would have been abrupt—Fine, No, and No—but Kelly was more diplomatic than I am in certain circumstances. Given how cranky she was just a few minutes ago, I was amazed at her level of composure. I just wanted to get to the results.

Dr. Swanson pulled up a picture on the iPad, showing us the tumor. It was blobby and just generally gross. And yes, it was about the size of a kiwi.

"Okay, now for the news you've all been waiting for. The tumor we removed has been classified as a meningioma, and it brings me great joy to tell you that it was benign."

Kelly put her hand up to her mouth in shock. I lowered my head into her chest and burst into tears. She put her arms around me, and we cried together, and I could hear Paige and Jackie doing the same at the foot of the bed. The doctor stood by and let us have our moment of joy.

Eventually, Kelly regained her composure enough to ask questions. "When can I go home?" I knew that would be her first order of business.

"As long as everything still looks good tomorrow, I think we can safely send you home, but it will be with some restrictions that you have to promise to follow. You did just have brain surgery, after all."

"I'll do whatever you say. I just want out. This place gives me the willies. What about follow-up treatment?"

"None to speak of except for annual exams. A very small percentage of meningiomas recur after a few years. We need to make sure you don't fall into that category, but we'll worry about that later. For now, just enjoy this good news. I'll be back in the morning during rounds, and hopefully, we'll get you out of here."

"Thank you, Doctor. Those words don't seem enough, but we have nothing else to offer you." I shook her hand. I wanted to hug her, but that didn't seem appropriate, so I refrained. After she left, I noticed Paige was in the chair, bent over with her hands covering her face. She cried softly while Jackie rubbed her back. I went over to her and knelt in front of her.

"Hey," I said, putting my hands on her arms. "Look at me. It's okay. It's over. We're not going to lose her, okay?" I wrapped my arms around her, rocking back and forth while she cried.

From across the room, Kelly said, "Paige, honey. Come here. Come sit with me." She wiped her eyes, blew her nose, and did as instructed. Kelly put her hands on Paige's cheeks and said, "Paige, I know what you're feeling, okay? This whole thing brought you far too close to those memories you spend so much time trying to forget. I'm sorry I put you through it, but Beth's right. It's over, and we can move on. I'll be around to butt into your life for many years to come."

Paige smiled through her sniffles. "You promise?" she asked.

"I promise."

I told everyone I was going out to get something from the vending machine. Instead, I went down to the ground floor and out into the courtyard. There was a fountain in the shape of what appeared to be an ancient Roman guy with a leaf crown on his head and water shooting out of a watering can he was holding. At first glance, the watering can was obscured by foliage, and it appeared as though he was peeing out the water. I couldn't imagine why they put it there, because it was really creepy, but the sound of the water comforted me. I realized I was breathing heavily and sweating. The crying had stopped, thankfully. Crying gave me a headache, which explained why my head had been pounding for the last four days.

I leaned over with my elbows on my thighs and took a deep breath, trying to slow my heart rate. I listened to the water with my eyes closed, practicing some measured breathing techniques I'd read in a magazine just a few days prior. When I finally seemed to have it under control, I looked up to see Jackie standing about ten feet away, just watching me. She came over, sat next to me, and handed me a cup of coffee.

"Is it just me, or is that a very disturbing statue?" Jackie put her hand on mine as she sat.

"It's not just you."

"You okay?"

"I'm getting there. It's taking me a minute to recover. I should be jumping for joy. But I can't seem to catch my breath. I'm not even sure why, to be honest."

"Isn't it obvious?"

"No. Why?"

"You almost lost her! A scare like that doesn't disappear when the tide turns and the news is good. When you realized how much you had to lose, it caused a seismic shift. You have to give yourself a chance to process all of that."

"I don't know what I would have done if..."

"You don't have to think about that anymore. The good news is that you get to take her home with a new appreciation for her."

"I don't know how I'll let her out of my sight after this."

"She's lucky to have you, Beth. Why don't we go back up there so you can enjoy this moment with your wife, huh? She's wondering where you went."

"I felt weak and vulnerable, and I didn't want to convey that to her and spoil her relief."

"I think you two are emotionally mature enough to navigate all those emotions—joy, weakness, and vulnerability. She'd rather have you up there with her than down here by yourself trying to shield her."

"When did you get to be so insightful?"

"I've done a little growing up recently. Perhaps you've finally noticed?"

"Thanks for helping Paige through this. She needed you."

"Not being here for her was not an option. I'm in it for the good and the bad from now on."

"You'll never hear her admit this, but Kelly is grateful too."

"I'm just glad I could help in some small way. Come on. Let's go see your wife." She grabbed my hand and led me back inside.

Chapter Thirty-Four

A WEEK LATER, PAIGE and Jackie were still in Atlanta, helping Beth care for Kelly at home. She was a terrible patient and wanted everyone to let her do things by herself, but since doctor's orders required rest and limited physical activity, she was at the mercy of her overprotective caretakers.

Beth had finally returned to work at the insistence of everyone in the house, and she'd only done so after writing two pages of Dos and Don'ts and tacking them onto the refrigerator. Kelly slept on the couch with the television volume turned low on an episode of *Friends*. Paige and Jackie sat on the bar stools at the kitchen counter, eating tuna fish sandwiches and discussing when they would be ready to go back home to D.C.

"I think I want to stay a few more days," Paige said. "I just don't feel ready to leave her now that Beth has returned to work."

"Paige, we can stay as long as you want, but her restrictions were only for a week from the surgery, and we're on day eight now. We have to start letting her do things. Her body needs to rebuild its muscle mass. She's ready. And she's irritated because we won't let her do anything."

Kelly slowly walked into the room and echoed Jackie's sentiments. "I never thought I'd agree with Jackie, but the moment has finally come. Yes, you all need to let me get back to normal. I'm fine. Yes, I'm weak, but I'm not going to get any stronger by laying around all day. And you two need to get back to your lives. Don't you have a wedding to plan or something? I'd love for you all to focus on something else besides me, please." She went to the refrigerator and took a lemon-lime LaCroix, drinking it from the can.

Jackie looked at Paige, smiled, and said, "You know she's cranky when she's encouraging us to get married to pull the attention away from her. I told you she was ready."

"Good point," Paige said.

"Paige, remember how you told me about a thousand times I need to stop being overprotective of you? It's time to take your own advice. I say this with love, but please go home."

"Ouch," Paige said, making a pouty face.

"Speaking of the wedding, have you two set a date yet? Keep in mind you have to wait for my hair to grow back. I refuse to be in any pictures looking like Demi Moore in G.I. Jane."

Paige walked over to Kelly and rubbed the fuzz on her head. "Well, grow it fast, please. I don't want to wait too long."

Kelly turned her attention to the mail on the counter. The medical bills were just starting to arrive, and she dreaded opening them. The envelope from Dr. Swanson's office was on the top of the pile. As she opened it, she saw a number in the five-figure range and immediately started to sweat. Reviewing the invoice, she looked at the amount due and saw $0.00. She found it impossible to believe that her insurance covered $35,345.00 in full, so she examined it more closely. Insurance covered $20,000. The next line item said *Payment received: $15,345.* Assuming there was some sort of clerical error, she opened the next bill from one of the laboratories. *Total amount: $6,350. Insurance paid: $3,000. Payment received: $3,350. Amount due: $0.00.* The third envelope was from Dr. Wilson, her primary care physician. *Total amount: $3,500. Insurance paid: $1,200. Payment received: $2,300. Amount due: $0.00.* In utter confusion, she pulled out her phone and called Beth.

"What's wrong?" Beth asked with panic in her voice.

"Nothing. I'm fine. Just confused. Did you mortgage the house without telling me or something?"

"What are you talking about?"

"I'm opening the mail. All of these medical bills, amounting to thousands of dollars, have all been paid in full. Where did you get the money for this?"

Paige and Jackie's ears perked up, hearing Kelly's side of the conversation. Paige started to speak up, but Jackie stopped her.

"Kel, I didn't pay them," Beth said.

"Then who did?" she asked.

"Your future sister-in-law." Kelly looked up from the stack of bills, seeing Jackie focusing her attention on her half-eaten sandwich.

"I'll see you when you get home." She disconnected the call without waiting for Beth to say goodbye and walked over to face Jackie on the opposite side of the counter. "Jackie, look at me." Jackie complied reluctantly. "What did you do?"

"I did what any good friend would do if they had the means."

"I can't take your money."

"You didn't take my money. They did." She pointed to the stack of bills on the counter.

"Jackie..." Kelly said seriously.

"Kelly..." she replied in a mocking serious tone.

"How did you even get these bills to pay them?"

"I made arrangements with the hospital to have everything handled."

"But this is thousands and thousands of dollars."

"It's not a problem, Kelly."

She looked at her sister for answers. "Did you know she was doing this, Paige?"

"I found out yesterday when I brought the mail in and saw all the bills. She wants to do it, Kel."

"So, let me get this straight. You have the means to just pay off..." She paused and did the math in her head. "Forty-five thousand dollars at the drop of a hat?"

"Wait til you see the hospital bill," Paige said, and Jackie shushed her.

"How much is the hospital bill?"

"It hasn't come in yet because the insurance company is still deciding how much of it they're going to pay," Jackie said.

"So you've seen the bill?"

"Yes," she said reluctantly.

"How much is it?"

"I'd rather not say."

"Jackie, it's my bill. You can't keep it from me."

Jackie sighed and pulled out her phone. She opened an email from the insurance company, discussing the negotiations of the final amount they intended to pay. Jackie clicked on the PDF of the invoice and showed it to Kelly.

"Another forty-three thousand?" she said incredulously.

"They'll probably agree to pay about twenty thousand of that."

"And you plan to pay that as well?"

"Yep."

"But...why?"

"Because I can. And I want to. We're family now, Kelly. Family takes care of each other, right? That's what you and Paige keep telling me." Paige looked over at Kelly and smiled.

"Is it true you hired a private jet to get Paige to the hospital quickly?"

"Yes. I didn't want her to have to wait to fly commercial. It was much faster to go private."

"So, just how rich are you, Jackie?" Kelly asked.

"Please don't make me answer that."

"Okay, okay. I won't pry. Sorry. I just...well, I'm speechless. I don't know what to say."

"Just say thank you," Paige said.

"Thank you, Jackie. I'm overwhelmed by your generosity. During the last few days in the hospital, when the surgery was over, I had so much time to think. I was trying to figure out how we would pay these bills. I had planned to refinance the house and hope that there was enough equity in it to cover what we needed."

"Well, now you won't have to worry about it. That's what money is for. It buys peace of mind." Jackie went back to eating her sandwich.

Kelly looked at Jackie and shook her head, trying to be mad at her. She walked around to the other side of the counter and went to Jackie, spinning her bar stool around to meet her eye to eye. "Thank you." She put her arms around Jackie and held her tightly.

Chapter Thirty-Five

A MONTH LATER, KELLY went back to work full-time. Her hair had grown back enough for her to feel comfortable being in public, even though I told her I really liked it buzzed and wanted her to keep it that way because I'd always wanted a butchy woman. I knew I was never going to win that battle, but hopefully, it made her a little less self-conscious about it while it was still all fuzzy. I don't think she appreciated the butchy comment, though. Kelly was many things, but butchy was not one of them.

We went out to dinner to celebrate her return to the real world. I toasted to her good health with a lovely cabernet, and we both agreed we were relieved beyond measure that this frightening chapter of our lives was finally over. As she was perusing the menu, I reached into my pocket and pulled out an envelope. I slid it across the table to her.

"This came in the mail today."

Kelly looked at it suspiciously, then noticed her sister's handwriting. She opened it to find the invitation to Paige and Jackie's wedding.

"I can't believe they're getting married in a month."

"I'm actually surprised they haven't eloped already. They're both impulsive as hell, so it seemed like a good bet." I waited a few moments to let this news sink in, then checked in on her to see how she was feeling about it. "So, what's your take on this? Happy or sad? Or mad?"

"Definitely not mad. I think I'm happy about it."

"You think?"

"Yeah. Jackie brings out mixed emotions for me, but I can't deny how happy Paige has been. And she certainly helped Paige through this brain tumor nightmare, so I'm grateful for that. Maybe she's growing on me."

"You will never hear the end of it if you admit that to her. Or to Paige, for that matter. If you'd like to maintain your air of 'pissed off older sister,' I suggest you keep that to yourself."

"Are you going to plan a bachelorette party for Jackie?"

"I've thought about it, but I'm almost afraid to have a room full of women at a party to tempt Jackie back to her former player lifestyle."

"Hmmm...actually, I like that idea."

"What? How can you possibly like that idea?"

"It's a test."

"Babe..."

"What?" she said, with an innocent look on her face.

"That's kind of mean, and it's a dangerous game to play."

"I disagree. If 'the new Jackie,'" she made exaggerated air quotes, "is really so reformed, let's see if she proves it to us."

"It feels sneaky," I said.

"Maybe it is, a little, but it's better to know before the wedding than after."

"So am I supposed to spy on her all night?"

"*Spy* is a very harsh word. How about 'keep an eye on' and see if she wanders into dangerous territory?"

"Are you going to do the same with your sister at her bachelorette party?"

"My sister doesn't sleep around."

"Your point is taken, but it still doesn't feel right. I don't want to set her up to fail."

"You aren't. I'm not asking you to pay a hooker to take her to bed. I'm just saying there are a lot of tempting situations in life and watching her in one of those situations is protecting your sister-in-law. There's going to be a room full of women, some of whom Jackie has probably already had some kind of a fling with. I'll feel a lot better about this marriage if I know she's keeping her hands to herself."

"I will agree to keep an eye on her. That's it. No setups, no strippers, no hookers."

"That's fair."

"Now, can we stop talking about them and focus on you? How was your first week back at work?"

"I'm exhausted."

"I knew you would be. I told you it was too soon. You're still supposed to be taking it easy."

"I'm not supposed to be doing physical stuff. Work doesn't count. I sit at a desk all day." She grabbed some bread, buttered it, and took a healthy sip of her wine.

"I know. I guess I'm just nervous about you doing anything. You've got that incision in the back of your head that scares me. A little too much exertion, and you're going to bust it wide open."

"Beth, you're being dramatic. The incision is healing very well."

"It's just...the rational part of my brain knows I can't keep you still in a safe bubble forever. Maybe it's taking me a while to loosen up because keeping you still is my way of controlling a situation that was out of our control."

"We haven't really talked about all you had to deal with while I was in the hospital. That's on me, and I'm sorry, honey. Had I been in your position, I don't know that I would have been able to be as calm as you were. Your composure under pressure was remarkable."

"I put on a good act. You didn't see me when I was alone."

"I should be mad at you for hiding your feelings from me, but under the circumstances, I know you did it for me, so I forgive you. Do you want to tell me about it?"

"Well, it's pretty simple. I've never been so scared in my life. The thought of losing you..." My eyes started to tear up, and Kelly grabbed my hand across the table. "I felt like I couldn't breathe. It's so easy to get complacent in our relationship. We move around day after day with every expectation that tomorrow is guaranteed. When that guarantee was taken away from us, I guess I lost some of my confidence. If we stay still, we're protected, right? Like I said, I know it's irrational."

"Is that why we haven't had sex since I've been home?"

"No, you were restricted from sex by the doctor."

"That ended a week ago."

"When did she say that?"

"When I called and asked her last week. I'm pretty sure I told you about that. I've missed you, and I wanted to know when we could be normal again."

"Maybe I tuned it out because I'm still scared."

"What is it that you're scared of?"

"Everything. Anything. The fragility of our existence."

"How can I convince you I'm fine now? We can't stop living just to avoid the one-in-a-million chance that something bad might happen."

"I know..." I said sheepishly.

"Do you still want me?"

"Of course I do. It's been almost six weeks. I miss you so much."

"Then stop missing me. Let's start off slow, okay? We don't have to have some wild S&M sex."

"S& M? Really? We've never done that. Not once."

"I'm trying to make a point. Just be with me. I miss my wife, Beth."

* * * *

When we got home from the restaurant, I could see Kelly was clearly exhausted despite her earlier comments regarding her desire to have sex. I suspected she was not going to admit it, so I debated giving her an out, but that could backfire because she might think I didn't want to be with her, which couldn't be further from the truth. I'd missed her terribly and had even resorted to masturbating a few times. Usually, I don't need to do that because we're pretty active when things are normal, but six weeks is far too long for me.

I wondered whether she had also taken matters into her own hands as the weeks progressed. Knowing my wife, doctor's orders would not deter her. She'd tried to convince me to have sex the first week she was home, and I had to lay down the law that it wouldn't happen until she was medically cleared, but as I confessed at dinner, even the doctor's blessing hadn't allayed my fears. Terror often takes precedence over desire, and that's what had been going through my head these last six weeks.

We climbed into bed, and her naked body clung to mine for the first time since the night before the surgery. We kissed softly, getting used to the feel of each other again. I ran my hands down her back and lightly scratched her with my nails. She kissed my neck, and I tilted my head back, encouraging her. Her lips moved up to meet mine, increasing in intensity, but I slowed her down, enjoying the soft, slow roll of it. I didn't want to go fast, and I didn't want to go hard. I wanted to revel in her, reacquainting myself with the feel of her.

I let my hands wander from her face to her shoulders and down to her stomach. She'd lost weight since the surgery, and her belly was flatter than I remembered. My fingers trailed slowly across each rib, making my way up to her breast, circling her nipple. I kissed her slowly, touching the tip of my tongue to her lips as she moaned. Her hand caressed my cheek, and she reached around my head in an attempt to pull me in deeper, but I resisted, insisting on this slow and steady pace. Her voice in my ear whispered in breathy tones.

"I've missed your touch so much," she said. "My body has ached for you. Please, baby."

"Shhh..." I said. "Trust me and let it build." I gently touched her nipple with the tip of my tongue as my hand flattened out on her belly. I let the palm of my hand glide over her entire torso, neck to hips, while I slowly kissed her breast. Her sounds of gratification increased in volume. She placed her right hand over my left and traced the path along with me. I put her hand on her nipple, making circular motions while I sucked on it. We took our hands and moved down past her hips, between her legs. I put my hand over hers and led her fingers onto her, circling her. We slowly caressed her, and I whispered, "I fantasized about this over and over these past few weeks."

"Oh yeah?" she asked in a deep, throaty voice.

"Yes. God, I've missed the way you feel and smell and taste." I breathed heavily as I spoke.

"Did you touch yourself while you were thinking of me?"

"Yes. I couldn't take the wanting anymore."

"Show me how much you wanted me," she begged, pushing my fingers inside her, thrusting her hips into my hand.

I slowed her down yet again, fucking her in a deliberate and steady rhythm. I let my tongue wander between her lips and her breasts. I felt her muscles slowly start to contract around my fingers, and only then did I finally increase my intensity to bring her to climax. Her body glistened with sweat, and she made glorious orgasmic murmurs and whimpers in my ear.

The magnitude of the moment overwhelmed me, and I could hear myself crying as I held her through the shuddering of our bodies. We caught our collective breath together, sinking deep into each other. She kissed my tears and dried them with her thumbs on my cheeks.

We held each other for what seemed like an hour, but it was probably only a few minutes before I could feel her start to relax in my arms and drift off to sleep. My body still felt electrified from the depth of emotions I was feeling. Fear, gratitude, vulnerability, and an overflow of love for Kelly that had reached a new upper limit—one I didn't realize was possible. I thought I was going to lose everything, but instead, I gained more than I deserved.

Chapter Thirty-Six

ON THE NIGHT OF the bachelorette party, I went to Jackie's hotel room to bring her down to the restaurant where the guests were gathered. We had checked in earlier that day, and my room was next to hers, in the spirit of the 'keeping an eye on her' plan. I felt like I probably would have booked adjoining rooms for us anyway, even if I wasn't in stealth mode, so I didn't feel too guilty about it. And with any luck, the only ones coming and going from her room would be Jackie and me.

I knocked on her door, and she let me in, half-dressed and still getting ready for the party. We were due downstairs five minutes ago, but I decided to cut her some slack. She looked great, even in her unprepared state. The suit she was putting on was a very dark blue with the slightest hint of piping around the edges of the collar and sleeves. Her shirt was pale yellow with very narrow, perfectly matching blue vertical stripes. She had a necklace in the shape of a heart with a diamond at the center. Very classy. I started to get worried when she topped off the outfit with earrings and a splash of her cologne. To say she looked attractive would be an understatement, and I might need to spend the evening warding the women away from her.

"You look, um...wow. You look fantastic," I said, as we were getting ready to go.

"What's with that look? You seem unhappy or maybe even surprised I look fantastic."

"No, no. Not surprised. Just wondering how all these women are going to keep their hands off you tonight."

"Relax, Beth. I'm not trying to impress anyone. It's a party, and I like to look nice. That doesn't mean I'm going to be flirting. You're dressed nice too, but you don't see me worrying about it."

"True, but you and I are different."

"You still don't trust me, do you?"

"No, I do." There was no confidence at all in my voice. "But, Jackie. If you think about it, you've only been with Paige for a few months. Forgive me if I'm still skeptical."

"Okay, so I guess my word isn't enough yet. I have to prove it. That's cool. You'll see. Come on. Let's go." She led us out of the room. I could tell she was a little upset with me, but I also think she wanted the chance to show me she had changed.

By the time we reached the party room, the music was already blasting, and people were dancing. When Jackie walked in, the guests started to applaud the bride-to-be. I heard comments from the party-goers about how Paige must be something if she's managed to get Jackie to settle down.

Jackie moved across the dance floor, greeting her friends as she went and dancing along the way. Someone had already put a drink in her hand. One woman, who I recognized as one of her former lovers, gave Jackie a full-on French kiss, then dipped her on the dance floor. We hadn't been there ten minutes yet, and someone was already making out with her. To Jackie's credit, she stopped the kiss as soon as it started, but still, this was going to be a long night. I was skeptical whether she would still shut that behavior down after a few bourbons.

I had arranged for buffet-style food service, and after about an hour of dancing and talking to the guests, I asked everyone to grab some food and have a seat. I made sure everyone had a drink in front of them, and I stood up, clinking my glass with my fork.

"Hi, everyone. I want to thank you all for coming. For those who don't know me, my name is Beth, and I'll be Jackie's best woman at the ceremony tomorrow." It was a pretty rowdy bunch, and they were already hooting and hollering before I even got started. "I'm sure those of you who know Jackie as well as I do are as surprised as I am that we are here tonight to bid farewell to her single life."

I paused to let the laughter die down. "But as someone who has been with her on this journey with Paige from the very beginning, I can say she is a changed woman."

I heard several women say, 'yeah, right!' and 'I'll believe it when I see it!' "I know, I know, I was skeptical too, but it's true!" Jackie was smiling, but also glaring at me from her seat next to me. "As you can see, I'm getting the side eye from her right now, but let's be honest, Jackie. You had to know this would be more of a roast than a tribute."

She laughed and said, "That's fair, I guess. I'm sure I deserve that!"

"Yes, Jackie. You've lived your single life to the fullest, but now, someone has finally captured your heart, and I, for one, couldn't be happier. As of tomorrow, you will legally be my sister-in-law, and I think that's pretty awesome. If I may, I'd like to offer you a little marital advice."

I heard lots of groaning in the crowd. "Bear with me. I'm serious. I thought about making this part of my speech like a comedy routine, but I think I'm better suited as your best woman if I mix it with a little bit of heartfelt advice. So, if you will indulge me for a few minutes."

I took a sip of my water, giving myself a few seconds to remember the notes I had jotted down. "For those who don't know this, Jackie's fiancé Paige is my wife's sister. Having known Paige for many years and knowing how alike they are, there are some tips and tricks for dealing with Gallagher women. The first is—they are always right. The sooner you accept this, the happier you will be. Number two—never, ever argue when she is hungry. You will regret that faster than you can say, 'Here, honey. Have a protein bar." And if you do make the mistake of picking a fight when she's hungry, you will take your life in your hands if you tell her she's only arguing *because* she is hungry."

Jackie laughed and said, "I've learned that lesson already—the hard way."

"The next piece of advice is important, and I mean this sincerely. I know Paige. I know what a big heart she has. It's been hardened a few times over the years, but whose hasn't, right? If you grab hold of that heart, cherish it, protect it, keep it safe, and most importantly, love it with everything you've got, then I can promise that what you will get in return will make you happier than you ever thought you could be." I raised my glass, looked out at the guests, and said, "Here's to you, Jackie. To you and Paige. Cheers!" We all clinked our glasses, and Jackie got up to hug me. "I love you, Jack. Don't screw this up, okay?"

"I love you, too. And I won't."

The party continued with a fair amount of drinking and dancing—probably more drinking than dancing, but who's counting? I watched Jackie and saw she was feeling no pain, but so far, she'd behaved herself. I knew some of the people at the party, so I did my job as hostess, and I mingled and chatted.

Everyone was taking pictures and videos, texting them to each other to share in the revelry. The guests started a very large group text thread, and before I knew what was happening, my phone was blinging off the hook with pictures. While I enjoyed seeing them, I was never particularly close to Jackie's friends when we were dating, so the idea of texting with them didn't thrill me. They seemed a bit immature, but in their defense, they were all younger than me, and it was a long time ago. It's not like Jackie was a model of maturity back then, either.

I was standing at the DJ table about to ask him to play *Hey Ya* by OutKast when something caught my eye, and I looked over at the coat room on the far side of the room. I saw Jackie, her hands on the hips of a very attractive woman whose face was moving away from Jackie after what had clearly been a kiss on the lips. I could tell by the tilt of the woman's head as she moved away. I recognized her as Sara Peterson, the barely post-adolescent girl Jackie had just broken up with when she showed up at our house for Christmas. They were talking intently, eye to eye, for some time, but I didn't see any additional kissing. I stood frozen in place, unsure of my next move. Should I pretend it never happened? Should I confront Jackie? Did I tell Paige and Kelly?

I took a seat to take some deep breaths to try to calm myself down. I didn't want to react angrily and make a scene in front of all these people. I decided to wait until the party was over, and we went back to our adjoining rooms. I vowed not to let her out of my sight for the rest of the night. She would not be going into that hotel room unless I personally saw her enter alone. My disappointment in her was profound.

I went to the bar and ordered a Coke, then spun my seat around so I could see what Jackie was up to. She was dancing with three friends. I noticed how they all were so touchy-feely with each other. Their arms were entwined together as if it was some prelude to a group sex party. It occurred to me as I watched that if I had seen the same group dancing ten minutes earlier, I probably would not be viewing it with such a critical eye. The seed of doubt had been planted, and I saw inappropriate actions everywhere I looked.

I imagined the conversation I would inevitably have to have with Paige. It was going to break her heart. And Kelly...oh my goodness. Kelly was going to kill Jackie. And me for telling her to give Jackie a chance.

When the guests finally started to leave, I took Jackie by the hand and led her back to the elevators to go to our rooms. As the doors closed and I selected floor ten, Jackie looked confused and said, "What's wrong?"

"What makes you think something is wrong?"

"Well, earlier in the night, you were happy and having fun, and then somewhere along the way, your mood tanked. What's up?"

"We'll discuss it when we get up to the room," I said briskly.

"You sound like a parent about to scold their child."

"Yeah, well, maybe there's a reason for that." The elevator door opened, and we walked quickly to her room. She was fumbling with the room key, and I grabbed it out of her hand to open the door.

"Okay, *Mom*. Would you like to tell me what this is all about?"

"I saw you, Jack."

"Saw what?" she said indignantly.

"I saw you kissing Sara. Over by the coat room. You had your hands on her hips as she moved away from you."

"I was not kissing her! I swear. Instead of accusing me, why don't you ask me what happened?"

"Okay. What happened?"

"She cornered me to talk to her. It was innocent at first, but then she started talking about how she missed me and how good we used to be in bed. She leaned in to kiss me. I was so unprepared for it, and it took me a second to react. If you saw my hands on her hips, then what you saw was me pushing her away. I did not kiss her back, Beth. I swear. As soon as I realized what was happening, I pulled away from her."

"How come you stayed there with her after that? Why didn't you immediately walk away?"

"Because I had to tell her how wrong she was. That we weren't good, and it was just sex. I told her I didn't even know what good sex was until Paige. I asked her to please leave me alone because I'm marrying Paige, and I will not do anything to mess that up. And *then* I walked away."

"I know you too well, Jackie. How am I supposed to believe you?"

"Because it's true. Look, I know I've been a cheater for most of my life. You, of all people, know that first-hand, but I swear to you. That is not me anymore."

"I feel like I have to tell Paige."

"What? Why? Please, Beth. Don't do this to me. Please! I didn't do anything wrong. You're going to ruin everything."

I so wanted to believe her, but my fears that the old Jackie was still in there were overpowering all other possibilities. "Let me sleep on it."

"Beth, the wedding is tomorrow! If you're going to tell Paige, I need to know about it. I need to make her believe me, even if you don't."

"We'll talk in the morning. Good night, Jackie."

* * * *

I heard Jackie pounding on my hotel room door at four in the morning. She was doing the thing drunk people do when they think they're whispering, but it's louder than their regular voice.

"Beth! Let me in. I need to talk to you." She pounded louder, and I quickly went to the door to let her in, hoping she hadn't woken the entire tenth floor.

"You're drunk, Jackie. What do you want?"

"Yes, I'm a little drunk, but this can't wait until I sober up. Otherwise, you're going to wreck my life. I need you to listen to me."

"I'm not wrecking anything, Jackie. You did this by making out with your ex-girlfriend."

"I'm telling you the truth. I did not make out with her. And I have proof."

"What proof could you possibly have?"

She pulled out her phone and opened up the group text with all of the pictures and videos. She found one of the videos, pressed play, and then handed me the phone. As I watched, she went over to the bed and sat down.

The video was loud, and I couldn't determine what was happening or why she showed it to me. It was long—probably three minutes—which in texting video time is an eternity. I was getting frustrated after about a minute, and then I saw what was happening in the background. It was the coatroom from a different viewpoint than mine, and I could see the encounter with Jackie and Sara.

Seeing Jackie's face from this angle, I could tell she was not enjoying this discussion. Sara put her arms around Jackie's neck, and Jackie pulled them away. They talked some more, then Sara tilted her head and leaned in. She kissed Jackie for less than two seconds, and Jackie put her hands on Sara's hips and pushed her away. This was the moment I had seen from the other angle—the hands on the hips and Sara's tilted head moving away from the kiss. She was telling me the truth. She didn't kiss Sara. She stopped Sara from kissing her. I watched the remainder of their conversation, and I could see Jackie emphatically making her point to Sara.

"Jack…" I said, embarrassed at my accusations. "I'm so sorry. I should have believed you." I walked over to where she sat on the bed and knelt in front of her. "Can you forgive me?"

"I thought you trusted me, Beth. I thought I had proven to you I've changed."

"You have. This is all on me. Maybe deep down, I wasn't sure you could change so much in such a short period of time, so I made assumptions and drew conclusions."

"Beth, listen to me. I don't think you understand just how much I love Paige. She's changed everything. I never wanted to be with just one person. I never wanted to get married. I never wanted to have kids. But I want to do every single one of those things with her."

"Kids? What? You guys are talking about kids?"

"Can we stick to the subject at hand, please? My point is the old Jackie died the minute Paige walked into your house on Christmas Eve. It feels like I'm some DNA mutation of my old self."

"Okay, that sounds really weird."

"Maybe so, but it's true. I swear to you I'm not going to do anything that will mess up my shot with Paige. I love her too much."

"I'm so sorry. Please forgive me. I thought I was protecting Paige, but in doing so, I thought the worst of you."

"Yeah," she said, lowering her head. I could see how hurt she was by my accusation.

"Can I still be your best woman tomorrow?" I looked at the clock by the bed. "Actually, today?"

"Yes. I forgive you. You get points for protecting Paige. I'm happy she has you and Kelly on her side." She paused for a second, then put her hand to her mouth in shock and said, "Oh, god. Please tell me you didn't call Kelly tonight and tell her this."

"No, I didn't. I wasn't sure what I was going to do, to be honest, but now I'm very glad I did nothing. It could have been a disaster."

"Oh, thank god. Kelly would not have believed me, regardless of the video proof."

"You're probably right." I paused. "Listen, it's four in the morning. You're going to be a wreck later. Hungover and exhausted. Why don't you try to get some sleep?"

"I'm too wired. What floor are Kelly and Paige staying on?"

"You can't see your bride before the wedding."

"That's just an old wives' tale."

"Why do you want to see her now?"

"I need to hold her, crawl in bed with her, tell her I love her."

"You really do, don't you?"

"I really do."

"Eighth floor. Room eight twenty-nine and eight-thirty. Don't go crawling in with my wife in eight-thirty, okay?"

Chapter Thirty-Seven

I WENT DOWN TO room eight-thirty after getting myself primped for the wedding. Jackie asked me to wear a light brown suit that wouldn't clash with her cream-colored tuxedo. I thought I was going to hate it when I saw it on the hanger, but I was quite pleased with the look once I had it on.

When Kelly opened the door, I saw her in her Donna Karan dress that was a similar shade to my suit but just a hair lighter, the perfect complimenting color. She looked gorgeous, and I had to pause for a minute to appreciate her.

"With the exception of the bride, there couldn't possibly be another woman at this wedding more stunning than you," I said, truly in awe of her.

"Thank you, baby. You're very sweet. And very biased."

"Biased or not, I'll bet I can find a dozen people who agree with me."

"Well, let's not take a poll, okay?"

"Okay. How's the bride doing? Nervous?"

"Not nervous at all, actually. How about the other bride? Hungover?"

"A little, yes. And a little nervous, too."

"Did she behave herself last night?"

"Absolutely. She got a little drunk, but nothing wrong with that. She seemed to have a really good time. And what about you guys? How was your party?"

"She also got a little drunk, but it just made her all gooey and happy. It was kinda fun to watch."

"Did everyone behave themselves?"

"Yes, I made sure of it."

"Of course you did, babe. I'm going to bring Jackie down. Is Paige almost ready? The guests are already assembling."

"We'll be down in about ten minutes." I kissed her and left the room, wishing I had time to do more than kiss, but that would have to wait. I had a bride to get to the altar.

I went to catch the elevator to go back up to ten, but Jackie was already there in the eighth-floor lobby waiting for me, ready to head down. She looked wonderful. The tux was gorgeous, and her green eyes and shoulder-length brown hair complimented it perfectly. She and

Paige were going to make a beautiful couple.

We got to the altar and took our places. I took a moment to remember my wedding day to Kelly. I was nervous as hell, but as soon as I saw her come down that aisle, my heart slowed to a steady beat, and I just knew everything in my life had led up to that glorious moment when my bride came to meet me. I hoped Jackie and Paige were feeling the same. Given what Jackie told me the previous night, I was confident she finally got it.

I looked over at her and found her staring at the door waiting for Paige to appear. Her mouth was ever so slightly opened as if she was already in awe of Paige before she had even entered her field of vision. The music started, and Kelly came down the aisle looking more lovely than when I'd seen her earlier. I smiled at her as she took her place.

Given how non-traditional Paige and Jackie were, I was surprised at how many of the usual wedding traditions they had incorporated into their ceremony. *Here Comes the Bride* began to play on the organ, and Paige appeared in the doorway. I heard Jackie gasp. I smiled as I watched her walk down the aisle, and when I looked over at Jackie, I could see she was already crying. I touched her arm as a show of support.

Paige's wedding dress was the same cream color as Jackie's suit. The color made the blue in her eyes pop, and I could see she, too, was tearing up. I wasn't sure what these two had planned for vows, but I would lay odds that neither could get through them without bawling.

Paige and Kelly's mom, Janet, walked her down the aisle in the absence of their dad, who had passed away about ten years prior. Janet's joy for her daughter was evident as they slowly made their way toward the altar. It was not going to be a religious ceremony, but altar still seemed the appropriate word for it since it was decorated with an air of reverence, minus the God factor.

Jackie had spared no expense in the preparations of this venue. You could never tell it was a ballroom in a hotel. Of course, it was the Four Seasons, so that helped. The female Justice of the Peace who would preside over the service did the usual 'we have gathered here today' speech, just as we had rehearsed it the previous afternoon, but as she spoke, she ad-libbed with her take on matrimony.

"Paige. Jackie. You are about to embark upon an adventure. Many of us here in this room have probably done the same in our lives; some successfully and others not. And while I'm not a marriage counselor, I've learned a thing or two about marriage, specifically

successful marriages. In my experience, those who have figured out
how to make this thing work have one thing in common. And it's not
love or even trust, surprisingly. It's respect. Respect for each other, for
the bond they share, for the families they share their lives with, and for
the holy grail that is every human being's ultimate goal—happiness. If
you ladies can figure out how to do that, you will find yourselves
laughing your way into senior citizenship, knowing you picked the right
person to take the ride with you."

She paused and looked at each of them. "Now...are there vows
to be read?" They both nodded their heads, and Jackie pulled her notes
from her suit pocket.

"Paige, my love." She looked down at the index card, pausing.
"You know what? I don't need this." She put the notes away again. "I
don't need notes to tell me what I want to say to you. All I need to do is
look into those gorgeous blue eyes, and it's as if all the pieces of the
puzzle finally fit, and I know exactly what to do. You've given me a
purpose in an otherwise meandering existence. I finally know where I
belong in this world—right next to you."

She choked up, needing to pause before continuing. Paige went
from teary-eyed to full-on weeping.

"Not long ago, I was fairly certain I would never want or need
anyone by my side. I had convinced myself that love was a Hallmark
Channel brainwashing, not a reality. Oh, my, was I wrong. You crashed
into me like a meteor, giving me everything you had right from the start.
You let me into that beautiful soul of yours and made it so I could never
be truly satisfied anywhere else. I hope with every ounce of hope I can
muster that I can be the partner, confidant, protector, lover, friend, and
most importantly, the wife that you deserve. I love you with all that I
am, Paige."

I handed Jackie a tissue, and she turned away from the guests to
regain her composure. I noticed Kelly had done the same for Paige as
she pulled out her notes.

"Well, I *do* need my notes in front of me because I have to make
sure I don't forget anything, and I'm not thinking very clearly right now."
She smiled, and we all giggled with her. "Jacklyn Marie Fairburn, I love
you. I love your confidence, your swagger, but I also love the
vulnerability that you share with only me. I love your voice, your eyes,
your hands. I love your intelligence and the way you use it without
making anyone else around you feel stupid or silly. I love that you were
willing to open yourself up to feelings you've pushed away in your past,

and you let me in." She wiped her nose and eyes as she looked at her bride, crying along with her.

"Someday, if we are very, *very* lucky, we will be sitting on our porch in our rocking chairs, with our gray hair and our wrinkled skin and arthritic knees. And I will look over at you and smile and remember that on this day, we vowed to grab on to each other and jump. And that was the best decision either of us had ever made. I love you, Jacklyn." I looked around to see tissues being handed out in every row. Even the Justice of the Peace and Jackie's uber-tough biker friends were weepy.

The ceremony continued, and I did my job as best woman, handing her the ring. Leave it to Jackie to find a simple gold band that somehow looked more exquisite than any other gold band. Once the rings were exchanged, and they were declared wife and wife by the powers that be, they kissed and laughed and held each other tightly while we all applauded.

I stared at my wife, watching her immersed in her sister's joy, her objections to this relationship finally laid to rest.

Chapter Thirty-Eight

I FELT A SENSE of deja vu as Jackie and Paige pulled into our driveway while we decorated the house with Christmas lights. The scene was the same as it had been two years earlier, but oh, so much had changed. Kelly and I walked to the passenger side, and we both grabbed Paige's hands to maneuver her and her very pregnant belly out of the car.

As the sisters hugged, I met Jackie at the back of the SUV to help with the bags. Much like that Christmas two years ago, the amount of luggage made me wonder if they were moving in.

"So, how does it feel to know you'll be a mom in a matter of weeks?" I asked.

"Absolutely terrifying. To think that I will be responsible for the survival of another human being...it's just insane."

"Lucky for you, you've got a pretty good partner in this adventure. She looks amazing, by the way."

"Doesn't she? I swear I wake up every morning, put my head on her belly to greet the little dude, and look up at her in amazement. She's growing a human! How can she do that and still look so beautiful? If I was carrying this child, you can bet I would look like I should have been thrown out with yesterday's trash."

"Knowing you as I do, I find that hard to believe, but anyway, I agree. She looks great, and that son of yours seems like he'll pop out any day now. She's huge!"

"Three more weeks to go. We debated not coming on this trip, but she insisted. Hopefully, she won't give birth in your living room." Jackie made her way to greet Kelly, and I went to see Paige. She had her hand on her belly, which, I imagined, was the default position these last few weeks while the baby was doing calisthenics in her womb.

My instinct was to reach out and touch her, but she was probably sick and tired of being touched, so I resisted the urge. I guess she could read my mind because she grabbed my hand and put it low on her belly so I could feel the baby kicking like crazy. I smiled and hugged her, feeling electrified by the visible and tangible signs of new life.

They settled themselves in the guestroom, then Jackie held Paige's hand as she waddled back to the living room. Jackie propped her up on the sofa, putting her feet up on a pile of pillows. I saw Kelly watching Jackie attend to Paige. Ever the protective sister, she stood close by in the event Jackie's care didn't meet with her approval. Paige caught her breath as she finally sat back to relax, her hand instinctively propped on her belly once again.

"What's a pregnant girl gotta do to get some of those home-baked cookies I smell?" Paige said.

"All in due time, Paige. They aren't done yet," Kelly replied. "I was hoping you and I could make a few batches together when you got here, but that baby seems just a little too ready to pop out for you to be doing that."

"I know I look like a cow, but honestly, he's not finished cooking yet. I've told him he has to wait until we get back to D.C."

"Since when do babies care what you think about their birth? He's gonna do what he's gonna do, and you have zero control."

"I plan to give birth to a very obedient child," she said, and we all laughed out loud.

"Good luck with that. In the meantime, is the nursery ready at your house?" I asked.

"Yes, Jackie's brother Kevin came to help us paint and decorate. We did a Sesame Street theme. It's adorable."

"You mean, your baby-daddy came over to help you paint and decorate the Sesame Street theme," Kelly said.

"Yeah," Paige said with a smile. "Him."

"I still can't get used to the fact that this child is going to have your DNA, Jackie."

"Sometimes I can't believe it either. Kevin has given us a gift. I'm not sure I'll ever find a way to thank him for it. It's the closest we could ever get to having a child together."

"Does he plan to stay in the baby's life as his daddy/uncle?"

"Yes. We've given him the choice, and he says he wants to be a dad. It makes me happy because I believe kids need a male influence. And Jackie and Kevin are so similar in personality. Kevin will be the male version of Jackie as his father. He has his own kids too, so the baby will have half siblings. Win-win."

"Have you decided on a name for the little guy yet?"

"Well, it's between David and Alex. The full names would be David Michael Gallagher Fairburn or Alexander William Gallagher Fairburn. What do you think?"

Kelly and I looked at each other and said, simultaneously, "Alex."

Paige smiled. "That's my favorite, too. Jackie's not quite on board yet, but I'm working on her." She smiled at Jackie as she spoke.

Jackie scoffed and said, "This is just the first of what I assume will be many parenting decisions we will disagree on. I'm trying to learn the fine art of compromise."

"Well, hopefully, your first two years of marriage have taught you a little about that," I said. "After all, you are married to a Gallagher." I looked at both Kelly and Paige and laughed.

"I'm a slow learner. Thankfully, Paige is very patient with me, but she eventually wears me down, so I think you can safely order AWGF monograms."

"We're not really the monogramming type. That's something you rich folks like to do," I joked. "He's just going to be Alex to us. And I love the sound of Aunt Kelly and Aunt Beth."

When Kelly and I learned Paige and Jackie wanted a child, Kelly had the same doubts about Jackie as a parent as she did about Jackie as a wife. I had to keep reminding her that their marriage seemed rock solid so far. In their once-a-week FaceTime calls, Kelly kept looking for cracks in Paige's armor, but so far, none had appeared. Jackie was loving and attentive, not to mention generous. Their assets were all put in both names, and true to her word, she refused to have a prenup drafted.

About a year ago, Paige had to tell Jackie to stop buying her expensive jewelry and cars because she had everything she ever needed and then some. As much as the skeptic in Kelly tried to find fault in Jackie, she was failing.

"So, speaking of Aunt Kelly and Beth, we have something we'd like to talk to you two about," Jackie said. "A favor, actually."

"Uh-oh," Kelly said.

"Now, now. Wait til you hear us out before you panic," Paige said. "We've been thinking about everything we need to do as parents to ensure that our son is loved and cared for. You know...contingency planning for all kinds of things, both good and bad. We're having our wills drafted, and we'd like to ask the two of you to be Alex's legal guardians if, God forbid, something terrible happens to us."

"Oh, geez, Paige. I don't even want to consider that possibility!" Kelly said indignantly.

"Well, we have to. Look, you could have died a couple of years ago, right? The same thing could happen to us. We just want to know for sure that Alex will be raised by the two people most suited to be his parents. And that's you two."

"I don't know what to say. I'm honored," I said.

"You don't have to answer right away. Talk it over together and let us know, okay?"

Kelly looked at me, and we smiled that knowing smile we have when reading each other's minds. I nodded, and Kelly said, "We don't have to talk it over. Of course, we will. As Beth said, I'm honored. We're honored."

Paige breathed a visible sign of relief. This must have been weighing on her. So many things to do when preparing for a child; it was as if she could mentally cross this one off her list.

"Oh, thank goodness. I feel much better now that we got that conversation out of the way."

"Were you worried we wouldn't agree to do it?"

"Not so much worried that you wouldn't agree, but worried you would say 'I don't want to talk about it,' and it would be left undone."

"I guess you know me pretty well, huh?"

"I've had a lot of practice being your sister, but I also knew you would agree, which is why we had our lawyer include you in the draft. Jackie has a copy for you to review when you have a minute, to make sure you agree to the way we structured it."

"What about Kevin? How does he feel about you choosing us as guardians?"

"He agrees, as long as he gets to maintain his relationship."

"Okay. All of this is a moot point, anyway. This is not going to happen. I seem to recall you telling me in the hospital that I was not permitted to die. Turnabout is fair play. This child is going to grow up in a loving household with *you two* as his parents and Beth and I as his aunts. End of discussion."

"Yes, ma'am." Paige saluted Kelly in mock obedience.

Chapter Thirty-Nine

AT TWO IN THE morning on Christmas day, Paige woke suddenly groaning in pain, but tried to keep her sounds to a whimper so as not to wake Jackie. The baby was pushing on her bladder, so she pulled herself up to go to the bathroom, only to collapse back down when the pain increased exponentially. Jackie awoke with a start and sat up, turning on the light to get her bearings.

"What's going on, honey?"

"It's nothing. Probably just Braxton-Hicks contractions. He's just practicing."

"Have you been timing them?"

"It's been erratic all night, but that last one was a doozy. Can you help me to the bathroom, please? I feel like a beached whale."

She came around to Paige's side of the bed and hoisted her up. Jackie smiled as they walked across the room. She loved Paige's pregnant waddle. It reminded her, in the most adorably visual way, that Paige had their future inside her body. The enormity of that responsibility caught Jackie off guard every time, but she pushed it to the back of her mind as she tended to Paige, focusing her energies on the moment at hand.

Paige took care of business, and Jackie hoisted her again, helping her back to the bed after Paige washed her hands. After two steps forward, they found themselves in a puddle as Paige's water broke. They stared at each other with mouths open, at a loss for words. Jackie blinked first, moving them along back to the bed. "Here we go," she said nervously. She quickly left the bedroom and headed down the hall to Beth and Kelly's room. Paige listened as the silence from down the hall quickly erupted into panicked conversation and scuffling feet. Kelly dashed into the bedroom and sat beside Paige, her arm around her shoulder.

"Paige, honey....um, do you recall a conversation we had a day or two ago when you insisted you plan to give birth to a very obedient child?"

Paige pressed on her belly and winced. "I do recall saying that, yes."

"Well, um...I think the boy is trying his damndest to prove you wrong. He wants to do things his way."

"I think I jinxed myself when I said that."

"Probably. In any case, we need to get you downstairs. Beth is trying to calm Jackie, who is just running around in circles, trying to figure out what to do first. Jackie! Come in here and pack up your wife's things, please!"

"There's a to-go bag over in the corner, all packed. We weren't going to bring it, but she insisted."

"Okay, honey. Let's get you up." Kelly grabbed her arm and pulled her to her feet. "Beth, come help me get her down the stairs. Jackie, come in here. Are you okay?"

Jackie returned to the bedroom looking as white as the duvet cover on their bed. "Babe," Paige said. "Everything's fine. Big deep breaths, okay? Can you grab my bag in the corner, please? And thank you for insisting that we pack it. Good call on that one."

When they came down the stairs, Jake and Ollie were riled up and barking from the excitement of their humans. Beth quickly let them out in the backyard to get them out from underfoot. Another contraction started, and Paige needed to pause for a moment before heading out to the car. Jackie came to her, and they had all four hands on her belly in a vain attempt to will the pain away. In his first act of defiance, the child was not cooperating.

* * * *

Once we made it to the hospital and settled them in their room, the debate about drugs or no drugs quickly became the topic of conversation.

Kelly said, "I don't think you should do it, Paige. Let yourself feel the whole process and let him come into the world with a clear head."

Jackie, unsurprisingly, had a very different point of view. "Drugs. Take them. Take as much as they will give you. If they give you one of those buttons where you can pump your own drugs, just keep pumping!"

Ever the mediator, I made sure I didn't offer a polarizing opinion. "I don't know, Paige. I can see both sides of the argument, and I think you should go with your gut."

"You guys are no help at all," Paige said. "I've got one No, one Yes, and one Maybe." She turned her attention to the nurse who was hooking up the fetal heart monitor. "Excuse me, ma'am?" She looked at the woman's name tag. "Cheryl, may I call you that?" Cheryl nodded in agreement. "Do you have children, Cheryl?"

"I do. Two boys and a girl."

"Great! So, absolutely none of my advisors here have been through childbirth. Their opinions are meaningless to me. Cheryl, what do you suggest?"

"Well, I had no drugs at all with my oldest."

"Okay, and what about the other two?"

"Drugs. Lots of drugs."

We laughed. "I think we have our answer," Jackie said.

"This is only my opinion, obviously. I get that you want to feel it all but trust me when I say you probably aren't going to enjoy it. It hurts like a..."

"Thank you, Cheryl. You've been most helpful. I'm going with the drugs, please."

"Coming right up!" Cheryl said.

* * * *

It took another six hours before little Alex decided to poke his head out into the world, literally. Paige handled it like a trooper, but Jackie was a wreck every step of the way. When we heard him exercising his newly discovered lungs, she cried as she wiped the sweat from Paige's brow and kissed her on the forehead. They let Jackie cut the cord, then placed him on Paige's chest. He wailed as they studied his face, whispering their love for him through their tears. Kelly and I stood back from the bed, letting the nurses do their jobs, and we cried together as well.

I watched as the midwife delivered the placenta, which was not a very pleasant sight, but all part of the process, so I wanted to bear witness to all Paige had endured. Millions of women do this every day, but it doesn't make it any less of a miracle. My heart exploded with joy for them.

They took the baby for a moment to clean him up and weigh him, but they quickly put him back on Paige's chest for skin-to-skin bonding. Seven pounds, twelve ounces, and twenty-three inches long. I counted his fingers and toes—all accounted for.

Jackie looked at him and then at Paige and cooed, "Hello, sweet Alexander William. Welcome to the world. We're your mommies, and we're going to love you *so* much. And look over there." She pointed to us. "Those are your aunts, and they will love you almost as much as we do. And they get to spoil you and then send you home to us."

We smiled in agreement, moving closer to get a good look at him. My maternal instincts started to kick in, and I looked at my wife with a fierce burst of what can only be described as a hormonal overdose. I felt flooded, literally, with a need to experience for myself what I witnessed from Jackie and Paige. I made a mental note to talk to Kelly about it later that day, but as I watched her, I suspected she was feeling the same, and perhaps this adventure would also be in our future.

This probably wasn't the best time to make that decision, but it was something to consider because the thought of Kelly carrying our baby was exhilarating. For the sake of Paige and Jackie, I put a pin in that thought and focused on little Mr. Alexander William Gallagher Fairburn.

I thought about the start of their journey just two short years ago. We unwittingly orchestrated the crossing of their paths, never dreaming it would result in a love story almost as perfect as mine and Kelly's. In the end, new life had emerged to start them on their journey as a family. Our family, unconventional as it may be, but a family nonetheless. I also thought about how funny life can be.

After decades of questionable choices, Jackie managed to see something in Paige from day one that led her down an unfamiliar path toward the greatest love of her life. Paige saw it too, and it allowed her to move on—finally—from the grief she had experienced so early on in her life.

I chuckled to myself, thinking that if either of them had listened to Kelly and me, we might not be here welcoming Alex into the world. He was here because these women knew what they wanted and went for it. I guess there's something to be said for that—for trusting your heart (and your gut) so completely that you fly away from the safety of what logic dictates you *should do* and fly into the potential chaos of the undiscovered.

As my wife and I cried happy tears watching the new family get acquainted, I think even Kelly would agree that things had worked out exactly as they were supposed to. I'm not so sure she would ever admit it out loud, but the look on her face said it all.

The End

About Barbara Lynn Murphy

Barbara Lynn Murphy is originally from Long Island, New York, but currently lives in suburban Atlanta, Georgia with her wife and five dogs. She is a late bloomer to writing, having only started doing so in earnest during the Covid years. What was once a passing fancy has morphed into a second chapter in her professional life (although she still maintains her day job in Technology—for now.)

Connect with Barbara:

Email: barbaralynnmurphyauthor@gmail.com

Facebook: Barbara Lynn Murphy

Twitter: https://twitter.com/BLMurphyAuthor

Instagram: https://www.instagram.com/barbaralynnmurphy/

Note to Readers:

Thank you for reading a book from Desert Palm Press. We appreciate you as a reader and want to ensure you enjoy the reading process. We would like you to consider posting a review on your preferred media sites and/or your blog or website.

For more information on upcoming releases, author interviews, contests, giveaways and more, please sign up for our newsletter and visit us at Desert Palm Press: www.desertpalmpress.com and "Like" us on Facebook: Desert Palm Press.

Bright Blessings

Made in the USA
Columbia, SC
18 July 2023

20179736R00098